Last Man Standing: Cordyceps

by

Keith Taylor

One Month On, A Nation Expects

Published May 4th, 2019 to the New York
Times website
Byline: Editorial Staff

In what's been described as the most
extensive mass migration event in the
nation's history, the month since the 4/7
attacks on New York City and Washington,
D.C. has seen millions flee west from the
once crowded eastern seaboard, both to
escape the immediate economic impact of
the disaster and to allay fears of further
attacks on major metropolitan centers.

An estimated 27 million refugees - almost
half the population of the now quarantined
northeastern region - have already escaped to
sparsely populated areas of Missouri,
Kentucky, Kansas and as far west as Oregon
in an exodus that has quickly overwhelmed
the capacity of municipal services, and local
governments have been left reeling under the
pressure to provide everything from

emergency housing and medical care to basic food and potable water.

"We're calling Lexington 'Manhattan West'," jokes Maria Sloane, a mother of three who fled to Kentucky along with an estimated 85,000 former residents of Paterson, NJ, in what has been claimed by some to be an unnecessary economic migration. The group has been temporarily housed in an emergency camp established on the outskirts of the Daniel Boone National Forest, where efforts are under way to find a more permanent solution. "There's lots of money coming into these poor states. I don't really get why they're so mad about it."

While Sloane is correct in saying that the last month has seen an unprecedented injection of capital into struggling flyover states - both from the direct infusion of wealth from new arrivals and generous federal subsidies aimed at relieving the immense burden on regional governments - patience is beginning to wear thin among local residents, with many concerned about what will happen when the cash and good will finally runs dry.

"I don't mind the people from New York or D.C. at all," claims Boyd Wilson, manager of a bait shop on the outskirts of Lakeview Heights, KY. "Those folks really suffered. If a man loses his home I'll throw open my door and offer him a roof, no questions asked, but I just don't understand why we're expected to take in all these other people." Wilson complains that new arrivals from areas broadly unaffected by the attacks have been overfishing the local Triplett Creek, and that Cave Run Lake in the National Forest has become little more than a playground for wealthy easterners who don't respect the sacrifices made by local residents.

"Just last week I had a bunch in here looking for tips on where's the best fishing down at Phelps Branch on the Creek. That's a protected stretch, I told them. They need a special license to fish there, but they didn't give a hoot. And these were Boston folk, I could tell by their accents. There ain't no problems in Boston, far as I've heard. Why can't they just go home?"

Despite the local tensions most would admit that the United States has weathered the storm remarkably well in the aftermath of these unprecedented attacks, with leaders from the United Kingdom and much of Europe praising the difficult but decisive action taken to quell the danger, and the compassionate provision of aid to those affected, using lessons painfully learned from previous catastrophes such as Katrina and Sandy.

There have, however, been strong criticisms both at home and abroad of the heavy handed approach of law enforcement and recalled military forces, including accusations of racial profiling in Baltimore that led to the tragic loss of scores of lives in last week's food riots. There have also been ongoing constitutional questions regarding the legitimacy of the federal government in the light of President Howard's ongoing incapacity and the death of Vice President Lynch. Speaker Terrence Lassiter's accession to Acting President, while recognized as constitutionally valid at the time, has now been called into question by those who claim that the crisis is over, and argue that the reins should be handed back to a Democrat.

The Acting President's fitness to lead is no doubt further challenged by the fact that his government continues to operate from Site R, the secretive underground command post in the Raven Rock Mountain Complex north of Camp David. Detractors have called this an act of cowardice unbecoming of the office, and the fact that the Speaker was broadly disliked on both sides of the political divide even before the attacks leaves him with few allies in the corridors of power. Many commentators argue that the President's refusal to appear in public or even speak to the media in the past week severely erodes the argument that he is equipped to guide the nation through this ongoing crisis.

But what may prove the downfall of the Speaker and his government are not the tensions in the refugee-swamped central states, nor questions of the legitimacy or efficacy of his office, nor even the approaching economic disaster following a month of closed borders and stifled global trade, but the growing disquiet over the continued detention of US citizens in Newark Airport's Camp One. The camp, established on the day of the attacks to house refugees from New York City, has found itself at the center of a controversy not seen since the internment of American citizens of Japanese descent in the 1940s.

Those of us at the New York Times understand more than most the terrible realities of war. All of us lost friends, family and colleagues in the attack on New York, and all who survived the attacks, from the deputy editor in chief to the staff in the mail room, know that sacrifices must be made. We know that if our great nation is to survive these dark times we can't shy away from actions we may not consider palatable in peace time, but the time for transparency has come.

Our questions are simple and direct: will this government admit that upwards of eight thousand healthy, uninfected American citizens have been used as test subjects to develop a vaccine or cure for *Cordyceps bangkokii*? Will journalists, inspectors and other interested parties be given permission to enter Camp One to investigate these troubling claims, and will those detained at Newark Airport be permitted to speak publicly about their time there? If not, why not?

The citizens of the United States demand that these questions be answered. For too long has Speaker Lassiter's government remained silent on this urgent and pressing matter.

They move closer to my cabin every night. I can hear the screams grow louder, echoing off the steel cabin walls, out across the runway and all the way back to my little cell where they rattle constantly through my mind. I think they took the people two rooms over last night. I can still hear the woman screaming.

The worst thing is that I don't have the first clue what's happening to them. I don't know where they're taken, and I don't know why. All I know is they scream and fight as they're dragged from their cabins. They're sure not going home.

I don't know how long it's been, exactly. I didn't start counting until the sixth - *seventh?* - day, and it was a couple of weeks before I started scoring a mark into the wall whenever they brought dinner, like an old timey convict. The days melt into one another so there may be a few in the over under, but I'm pretty sure it's been around four weeks.

Four weeks since I lost my home. Four weeks since I last saw a TV or read a newspaper. Four weeks since I stood beneath a shower. A real shower, I mean. Not the warm, sudsy drip from a sponge moistened in the bucket I shared with Bishop and Edgar, at least until the old man was taken away. Now the two of us get the bucket all to ourselves, each turning to face the opposite wall as the other cleans himself as best he can, rinsing the soap suds into the sluice by the chemical toilet. They only fill the bucket once a day, so each day we alternate who goes first and who uses the dregs. Luxury.

They started taking blood the first couple of days. A precaution, they assured us, to make sure none of us were infected with a slow burn before they release us. 'Slow burn'. That's what they call an infection from a non-fatal injury. They say it can fester in the wound for a while before it finally works its way into the bloodstream and reaches the brain, but I don't buy it. I don't buy any of this shit. They did a head to toe examination of all of us on the first day, and they already know we don't have any wounds caused by the infected.

It didn't take long before I began to suspect they were drawing our blood to keep us worn out, sluggish and docile. It all adds up. We're anemic. The food is bland and low energy. We constantly feel sweaty and gross. It's the perfect formula to sap our will to do anything. All I want to do is lay in bed and stare at the ceiling. We're ideal prisoners.

It was the day they dragged Edgar away that I really started to worry. He was just a sweet old man from the Lower East Side, one of those guys who lived in the same little rent controlled apartment for forty years, even after everyone they know has moved out. Even after a bunch of middle class hipster pricks like me moved in to replace them, buying up entire blocks and opening overpriced boutiques and Starbucks franchises, like yuppie parasites. New York used to be full of Edgars, and this guy was no different than the rest. He liked cats, he thought my generation was a little soft around the middle, and he tried to explain the rules of Bridge. He was harmless. Wouldn't hurt a fly.

That's what made it so weird to see the old man take his final breath through a bubble of blood.

Edgar was already there when Bishop and I were assigned to his room, a couple of days after we arrived when they shuffled us from the tents to long rows of prefab steel cabins with heavy walls and thick doors. He'd set himself up on the cot closest to the door, the first in two rows of four, and he'd already made his little space his own with photos of his late wife and a few books he'd been carrying in his bag when everything went to shit.

I laughed the first time I saw him. I didn't mean to, but it was just so funny to see this wizened, stoop shouldered old guy dressed in oversized army fatigues. He looked like a Captain America experiment gone wrong, peering out at us through a pair of thick milk bottle bottom glasses that made him look like an owl.

I felt bad for laughing as soon as he jumped up from his cot and tried to make us as comfortable as possible. I was supporting myself on Bishop's shoulder as we walked in, still a little weak after losing so much blood and my face stitched up like I'd taken shrapnel, and Edgar couldn't have been nicer. He even offered to move to a different cot so I could take the bed closest to the toilet by the door. He seemed relieved when I turned him down with a smile, and explained to us in graphic detail about the kidney problems that forced him to get up three times a night to use the john. Still, it was kind of him to offer.

That's just what he was: kind. In the two weeks I knew him he didn't have a bad word to say about anyone. He was pleasant with the guards, even after they told us we'd have to be confined to the cabin for our own safety. Even when they stopped letting us sit out on the runway to feel the sun on our backs. Even after they started locking the doors, and the guards started coming on shift armed with M16s rather than just standard sidearms. He just lay there and quietly read his books.

And then he started to get agitated one night a little after dinner, without any warning at all. It was as if a switch just tripped in his head out of nowhere. Nothing much was going on. I was tossing playing cards across the room into a bowl, Bishop was laying on his bed staring at the ceiling, and Edgar was quietly leafing through some dog eared old book when suddenly he slipped a bookmark between the pages, set it down, climbed out of bed and strode over to the locked door.

"I'd like to come out now," he calmly called, tapping his knuckles against the steel. "Guard? *Guard*. I said I'd like to come out now."

I heard boot soles crunch on gravel as the guard walked down the row towards our cabin, and he appeared at the door with a scowl. It was Lewis, the same guy who'd ridden into the camp on the truck with me and Bishop. Sweet kid. He kept us in cigarettes.

"Go back to bed, Mr. Klaczko," Lewis spoke softly through the chicken wire that covered the small open window in the door. "Lights out in ten."

Edgar banged hard on the door as Lewis began to walk away. "You don't understand,

I need to come out! I gotta get out now. Open the door." He slammed the heel of his palm hard against the steel, shaking the door in its frame. "*Lemme out*!"

Lewis looked a little shaken at Edgar's sudden outburst, and he kept his eyes fixed on the old man as he tugged his radio up to his mouth and called for backup. As he dropped it back down to his chest he swung his rifle off his shoulder and held it defensively, pointed towards the ground but ready to raise the barrel at any moment, as if this fragile old guy could possibly break the door open. "Back away from the door, Mr. Klaczko. Back away *now*. I won't tell you again."

Edgar didn't even seem to register Lewis' presence. He just kept punching against the locked door, yelling to be let out until his voice broke into a plaintive cry. It was only when he started tugging at the chicken wire that I rolled myself off the bed and walked over to help, and by the time I reached the door Edgar had gripped it so tight his fingers were bloody.

"Come on, Edgar, it's OK," I said in a soothing voice, reaching out to his bony shoulder in an effort to gently pull him back towards his cot. I didn't see the elbow coming. Didn't even feel it as he drove it hard into my nose like a piston. The next thing I knew I was on my ass, my ears ringing and my vision blurred with tears, my bloody nose squashed against my face like an overripe tomato.

I think I may even have passed out for a moment, like a pussy. I couldn't really tell, but all I know is that one second the door was firmly locked, Edgar still tugging desperately at the chicken wire with his bloodied, clawed fingers, and the next it was wide open and the cabin was swarmed with soldiers. They weren't soldiers like Lewis, the fresh-faced young private in carefully pressed fatigues who acted more like an overworked hotel concierge than a grunt, but terrifying black clad fuckers wearing anonymous face masks and knives strapped to their thighs. They looked like the kind of guys who'd go for a piss in tactical formation.

I remember the blow. Edgar rushed for the open door, yelling in a voice that had gone far beyond words. It was just a mournful, keening wail, as if he already knew he'd never reach the freedom he so desperately craved, broken off when the guy standing beside Lewis took a step forward, swung his gun around and drove the butt firmly into the old man's face. Maybe I only imagined hearing the crunch of bone and cartilage. I don't know. What I do know is that Edgar, an 84 year old bag of bones clothed in pale, papery skin, fell to the ground beside me like a sack of potatoes. For a moment a bubble of blood grew on his lips as he let out a breath, and then it burst into a trickle that ran down his gray, wrinkled cheek.

He didn't breathe again. I watched him for a long moment in the stunned silence and his chest didn't move. The thick blue vein in his throat didn't pulse, and his body was still. He wasn't just out cold. There was no coming back from where he'd gone.

One of the soldiers grabbed me by the hair and dragged me towards the back of the room while another trained his rifle on Bishop, still frozen on his cot. In front of me a couple more hooked their arms beneath Edgar's and dragged him out of the room while the rest backed out slowly, their guns still raised, filing backwards through the door and locking it quickly behind them.

We didn't see Lewis again after that night. He was replaced by a group of soldiers we hadn't seen before, each of whom spent an hour or so guarding the cabin door until a workman came along in the morning and switched the bloodied chicken wire in the window with a sheet of steel.

That was the last time Bishop and I felt the breeze. That damned steel plate blocked off our last connection with the outside world, and for the last two weeks we've been stuck in this hot, humid, stinking sweat box with nothing but Edgar's collection of old photographs, a stack of his dog eared books and, over by the door, visible from every corner of the room and weighing on us both even when we're not looking at it, a patch of carpet stained dark with his blood.

May 12th(?) 2019

It takes me a moment for my brain to get into gear when I hear the voice. "Hey, Tom?" I turn to Bishop's cot, surprised to hear him speak. He hasn't made a sound since burping after breakfast this morning.

"Yeah, what's up?" My own voice cracks a little. My throat is dry and scratchy, and I realize I also haven't spoken for hours. It feels good to hear something other than the wind buffeting the sides of the cabin.

"I've been thinking," Bishop continues, his words plodding out slowly in a tone I've come to recognize as meaning he's about to say something stupid, "ain't it weird that, y'know, lots of famous people have probably turned into those things?"

Huh. Compared to his usual nonsense that's not all that bad. "Yeah, I guess. I haven't really thought about it, but yeah, I supposed some of them must have."

Bishop raises himself up on his elbow to face me. "It's weird, right? I mean, just imagine you're walking down the street somewhere in Manhattan, just minding your own business, heading out to buy a pack of smokes, and, like... I don't know, John Lennon or some shit comes running around the corner all batshit crazy, and you're like '*holy crap*, I'm gonna have to kill John Lennon!' It'd be weird, y'know? Like, imagine if he was your favorite singer and you didn't know if you could kill him, and you're wondering if you should just let him get you. Y'know, outta respect or something."

I peer over at Bishop and try to read his expression. Even after all this time locked up together I can't quite figure out if he's really this dumb or some kind of expert troll, just playing with me for kicks.

"You know John Lennon died, right?"

Bishop's eyes grow wide with surprise. "No shit! In the attack?"

"In the— no, like thirty years ago! You never heard that? He got shot outside his apartment. It was global news!"

Bishop sighs and drops back to his cot. "Well God damn, ain't that a kick in the sack? I really liked that guy." He stares at the ceiling for a long moment as I watch him, looking for a telltale smile that might give it away that he's kidding, then he starts to sing under his breath. "*All my bags are packed, I'm ready to go... I'm standin' here outside your door... I hate to—*"

"Are you fucking with me, Bishop?" I demand, halfway between amused and mad.

"What? No! What do you mean?"

I swing my legs off the bed and stare at him, determined to figure this out once and for all. "I mean you're singing a fucking John Denver song. He died years ago, too. Now, are you messing with me?"

Bishop frowns so hard his eyebrows almost meet in the middle. "So who was the guy in Full House?"

"John Stamos. Not a singer. He's... fuck it, he's dead too. All your favorite Johns are dead. All the Johns are dead. There are no more Johns. Now go to sleep, you jackass."

I push myself off the cot, fumble in the jacket pocket of my fatigues for my cigarettes and sigh as I open the half crushed pack. I only have three left. Lewis stopped delivering smokes when he was taken off guard rotation after the Edgar incident, and the new guys refuse to bring us anything other than food and water. I had half a carton stashed under my bed back then, but unless the guards suddenly decide to get real friendly Bishop and I will both be climbing the walls by tomorrow.

I light up the battered, wrinkled Marlboro, take a deep pull and blow the smoke towards the spinning extractor fan in the wall beside the door, wishing I could follow the smoke outside as the fan grabs it and whisks it away. Wishing I could feel the breeze. That I could get the fuck out of here, away from that patch of blood and the still, sweaty, stifling air. That I could find out what the hell's going on outside these walls, and why we're still locked up in here.

I can't deny that the last month has taken its toll on both of us. Neither of us talk much any more. Neither of us can sleep through the night. Bishop seems to be handling it a little better than me - he seems blessed with a blissful lack of imagination that insulates him from the horror - but even he isn't his usual chatty self. When he bothers to speak his thoughts are usually about death these days.

As for me, I can't help but play a constant game of 'if only.' *If only* I hadn't trusted Sergeant Laurence, Kate might still be alive. *If only* we hadn't met Arnold we might have driven straight to the bridge instead of the park, and Kate might still be alive. *If only* I hadn't given up my obsession with the warning of the attacks I would have taken us out of the city that week, and Kate might still be alive. Hell, *if only* I'd just followed through on my plan to learn how to be a real man I might have bought some shack out in the woods, far from danger, living off the fat of the land. I'd have never met Kate, and I wouldn't give a damn if she were alive or dead.

But those thoughts all lead me back here to the grim, inevitable conclusion. I can obsess about a million what ifs, but the only thing that matters is the reality. I didn't do any of those things. I was dumb, lazy, feckless and irresponsible, and now I'm trapped in a steel box and Kate is just another corpse buried in the ruins of New York.

I blow another plume of smoke into the fan and feel a cold sweat beading my brow as I notice the layer of dust built up around the blades. I'd swear it grows thicker by the day, and I can't help but imagine that it's ash from the city, blowing our way whenever the wind shifts, carrying tiny particles of a million burned, rotting corpses towards us. We're surrounded by it, breathing more of it in with each breath, shifting the balance in our bodies just a little more each day from alive to dead as the dust builds up in our lungs, choking us. It makes me—

Hang on.

"Bishop," I whisper, turning my head so I can better hear the distorted sounds filtering through the whirring fan blades. "Did you just hear an explosion?"

Welcome to Newark International Airport. The green sign still marks the entrance but it's now obscured by another, more forbidding notice that stands in front, its black letters printed against a red background.

You are now entering Camp One. Entry permitted to authorized personnel only. Deadly force will be used beyond this point.

The sniper takes a slow breath to calm his nerves, exhaling through pursed lips, waiting for his thumping heart to slow.

"Just take your time, Warren. We've got all night. We can wait as long as it takes. Do you need anything?"

He looks up from the scope with an impatient scowl. "I need you to shut up and let me focus, Vee, OK? I've never committed treason before, so I'd like a minute to get used to the idea."

Victoria Reyes nods silently, biting her tongue as Warren shifts uncomfortably on the asphalt, returns to the scope and delicately adjusts the reticle.

The ghostly image of the guard glows green in the scope, illuminated by the light inside the guard post. It should be an easy shot with his trusty M40A5. Just 200 yards or so to a well lit, unobstructed target on a level plane, with nothing more to worry about than a gentle, steady tailwind. A novice could make this shot on his first attempt with a well-calibrated rifle - and Warren tends to his like a father to his son - but still his hands tremble. Once he squeezes the trigger there's no going back. He'll be a traitor to his country, and a traitor to the Corps. Seven years of service to - and a lifetime of love *for* - the United States will be wiped out in an instant. He'd never be able to explain this to his father, rest his soul.

He takes another breath and clears his mind. There's no point worrying about it any more. He knows what he has to do, and he knows this is the right thing, even if it feels wrong. The decision was made days ago, and the facts remain the same now as they were then.

A final breath. His pulse slows, and he finally finds his way to that cool, focused part of his mind he keeps locked away from the rest. The simple, analytical place that doesn't care about anything but wind speed, distance to target, air temperature and humidity. He exhales, pauses, gently squeezes the trigger...

The guard drops out of sight a moment later. A clean head shot through the open window. Warren smoothly pulls back the rifle, snaps the cap back on the scope and surveys the scene. In the distance off to the right he watches a couple of guards patrolling the outer perimeter, heading away from the entrance. They keep up their slow pace along the outer fence. They didn't hear the shot. He knows from watching them over the past few nights they've become complacent and lazy, and they won't be back for at least twenty minutes. Maybe longer, if they decide to stop for a smoke along the way.

"OK, let's move," he whispers, slipping the rifle over his shoulder and hopping the low wall that was hiding them from view. Vee takes the lead, sticking close to the cover of the wall with her M16 at the ready, her finger hovering close to the trigger. Security has been light in the area thanks to the fact that almost everyone who lived within fifty miles of New York is either dead or hunkered down in camps hundreds of miles to the west, but there are still occasional random patrols on the service roads that surround the airport. This is no time to get overconfident.

Vee reaches the guard post first and ducks her head through the door to make sure the guard is down for good, and Warren follows her in to take the pistol and radio from the guy's body. There's no remorse now. No guilt. What's done is done.

Warren twists the volume dial on the radio to its lowest setting and clips it to his jacket collar, keeping one ear listening for chatter as they move deeper into the airport complex. Neither Vee nor Warren bother to speak. There's no need for it. They've both seen the satellite photos, and they both know exactly where they're headed: the runway.

He breathes a sigh of relief as they reach a maintenance building on the road to the main terminal building and find just what the photos suggested would be waiting for them. A bank of electric courtesy vehicles are parked up in an open garage bay, all hooked up to recharging stations that have long since run out of power, and from a row of hooks on the wall hang bunches of keys attached to chunky bright yellow fobs. Vee grabs one at random and tries each vehicle until the third starts up with a quiet electric hum.

"Thank Christ for that," Warren sighs happily. "I wasn't looking forward to setting the charges close up." He hops into the passenger seat and sets down his rifle while Vee slides into the driver's seat and pulls the cart from the bay.

The hum of her motor and the sound of rubber on asphalt are the only things that break the silence as the cart rolls through the darkness along the service road that runs around the east end of the main terminal building. It's far from the quickest route to the runway, but it's the only one that isn't bathed in bright floodlights and regularly patrolled, an oversight Warren knows will cost the assholes running the base dearly. This is what happens when you pull out dedicated, well trained soldiers and replace them with private thugs who are paid by the hour: you get fucked.

A mesh gate bursts open as they power through it and out onto the apron, the black asphalt crowded with hastily abandoned service vehicles that litter the area in the shadow of the silent terminal. Thousands of prepackaged airline meals rot in delivery trucks that have long since lost their refrigeration. Luggage trains snake between the planes, their contents strewn across the ground where they were abandoned in the rush for the ground staff to escape.

Even after a month this shit still amazes Warren. It seems crazy that if the mood struck he could pull over and spend a couple of hours picking through the belongings of a thousand passengers, helping himself to laptops, tablets, cellphones, cash and jewelry that have been sitting here unattended for a month, like the world's best yard sale. Back in the first week he actually did grab a few tempting shiny objects while sweeping abandoned homes and stores with the cleanup crews on Staten Island. It was fun for a while, but it didn't take long before he realized there was just no point in owning luxury shit any more.

It was a commercial that brought it home to him, back at the end of the first week when the networks were still running regular programming as if they were trying to convince themselves that the world could never *really* go to shit as long as reruns of Everybody Loves Raymond ran as scheduled in the TV guide.

Warren was back at base, shoveling a rank jambalaya MRE down his throat, trying to ignore the stink of death that clung like tar to his clothes and worked its way up his nose, when a commercial for Omega wristwatches caught his eye. Black and white, real classy shit. Some buff guy with thick hair and just the right amount of stubble rocked up to a jetty to find a hot chick waiting for him on the deck of his yacht. She seemed to be enjoying spontaneous multiple orgasms at the very thought of this smug asshole climbing onto the boat, then the camera moved in to show his wrist. Omega Seamaster. Regular aspirational bullshit. Buy this watch and your life can be just as awesome as this.

Warren looked down at his own wrist and saw the exact same fucking watch. Brushed stainless steel, automatic movement, beautifully smooth chronograph. $4,500 of luxury, and he'd taken it from the wrist of a guy who was lying dead beside a classic Bugatti parked in the driveway of his palatial home, beaten to death by a woman who was probably his wife. Warren had put her on the ground with two shots from 100 yards, then he'd put a bullet in the guy's head just to be safe.

The watch hadn't done much for that guy. It hadn't allowed him entry beyond the velvet rope into the exclusive, perfect, endless hedonistic life he'd been promised by the commercial. It probably hadn't made women go wild with desire at the very thought of him. It had just made his chubby, torn up corpse a more attractive target for looters. All that aspirational shit's done. Over. You want to aspire to something? Get a decent gun, and aspire to still be alive in the morning.

The cart rolls silently out towards the runway, weaving between abandoned jets that had been waiting for a takeoff slot when the airspace was closed. The doors are all wide open, each of them spilling out bright yellow deflated emergency slides. Each of them carrying the names of airlines that haven't landed in the States for a month, and probably never will again: Emirates, Qantas and British Airways, all more than happy to abandon millions of dollars of aircraft and equipment if it means they can help keep this shit from spreading any further.

Of course, that's exactly what the pricks running this camp *want* to happen. That's the only reason this fucking place exists. That's why Vee and Warren are taking such a risk.

"OK, you ready for this?" asks Vee, holding the steering wheel steady with her knees as she tugs a large block of C-4 from her pack and pushes a blasting cap into the mass.

"Ready as I'll ever be," Warren replies, taking the C-4 from her hand and securing it firmly to the dash. He prepares himself to roll as Vee guides the cart towards the target. She sets the perfect approach angle, and Warren swings his rifle against his chest as they draw closer to the cover of an abandoned fire truck.

They both roll as one away from the vehicle, quickly pulling themselves to their feet and ducking behind the truck as the electric cart continues on towards the target, the accelerator wedged to the floor. Vee grasps the remote firing detonator in one hand and steadies her M16 with the other, waiting for the right moment.

Under the harsh floodlights lining the runway the courtesy vehicle rides silent, straight and true towards the first of three banks of dark green prefab cabins that extend at least a half mile down the runway. There are hundreds of them, maybe even a thousand, all of them powered by a tightly packed cluster of hybrid solar-diesel generators humming away at one end. The cart approaches them. Fifty yards. Forty. Thirty. Warren whispers a prayer as the cart begins to pull a little to the left. Twenty. Ten. It's slightly off target, but it looks like it'll still strike close enough to count.

Vee flips the cap on the detonator and squeezes the trigger.

All hell breaks loose. The rain-soaked black surface of the runway glows for a brief moment with the reflected flash of the explosion, and a fraction of a second later the truck rocks to the side as the shock wave passes and the noise washes over them. Vee and Warren wait for the roar to pass, peer around the side of the truck and smile when they see they've achieved their goal.

The bank of generators lies in ruins. The burned out wreckage of the cart smolders, while around it lie piles of twisted steel and shattered solar cells.

The floodlights flicker and fail for a moment as they switch to their own emergency solar charged backups, returning at half power and casting the runway in an eerie half light. It's dim, but in the ghostly glow Warren sees the result of the destruction.

The electronically locked doors at the front of each cabin swing slowly open under their own weight.

I stare at the open door in disbelief, wondering for a moment if my mind hasn't finally cracked under the pressure. I haven't seen the door open without an armed guard standing behind it in two weeks. I'd almost forgotten what the empty runway behind it even looked like.

It's only the burned down cigarette between my fingers that drags me back to the moment. I drop the butt to the steel floor and turn back to Bishop, sitting at the edge of his cot in the sudden darkness, staring open mouthed at the door as if he's waiting for me to confirm that he's not imagining it.

"Wait there," I whisper, holding my hand out to keep him on the bed. "Lemme check it out." I don't want us to go rushing out only to find ourselves pushed back in at gunpoint. I don't think ether of us could face that. Not after taking our first breath of fresh air in two weeks. I edge closer to the door, sticking by the wall until I can just about see out onto the runway.

"*Fuck!*" I jump back as the sound of gunfire breaks the silence. Muzzle flashes reflect off the dark steel of the door, and I hear the rapid drumbeat of automatic weapons fire striking the side of a nearby cabin. Whoever's firing, it's close.

It's also panicked. The rate of fire suggests someone burning through his magazine far too quickly. These aren't the quick, controlled bursts of a trained soldier. They're the frantic, last ditch shots of someone who knows he's about to die.

"Get back, Tom," hisses Bishop, rolling behind the cover of his cot. "Don't go out there!"

Yeah, no fucking kidding. I don't know what the hell's going on outside our door, but it doesn't matter. There's no way in hell we could ever make it across the hundreds of yards of open space outside the cabin. There's zero cover, and picking us off would be like shooting fish in a barrel. It's probably safer to take shelter at the back of the room and wait for the chaos to end.

I'm halfway across the room when I hear the sound echoing between the cabins.

Snarling. Groaning. Rasping breath.

I freeze mid-step, holding my breath as I listen for the sound again. That's a sound I've heard before. It's a sound forever burned into my memory, and I've spent the last month hoping against hope I'd never have to hear it again. It's the sound of approaching death.

"Bishop," I whisper, scanning the room for anything I could use as a weapon, "we need to get the fuck out of here, *now*." I almost expect to have to coax him out from his hiding place but I'm surprised to see him stand, lift his bed easily onto its side and begin to unscrew one of the thick steel legs from the frame. It comes loose in just a few seconds, and he tosses it over to me before grabbing another.

"I figured we might need to use these for a breakout," he shrugs, noticing my surprise. "I think they're full of sand or something. Could make a good cosh, you know? I noticed they screwed off a few days ago."

I swing the pipe experimentally, surprised at the weight. Bishop could be right. There's definitely something inside the hollow tube, and it feels solid enough to at least get in a good crack if it comes to it.

"Good thinking, Bishop. OK, you good to go?" I ask, still surprised that he isn't cowering in the corner.

"Does the Pope shit in the woods?" He tugs on his jacket and makes for the door. "I've been good to go for a God damned month. Let's get the fuck out of here."

Outside the door the floodlights spaced between each cabin flicker dimly, struggling to maintain their power. Small pools of light illuminate the outer walls of the cabins, but between them deep shadows hide God knows what on this moonless, cloudy night. I flinch as a shot rings out somewhere behind me, and in the darkness I hear frightened yells and hissed whispers from the people still hidden in the cabins. Nobody else seems to have dared emerge yet, and for a moment I wonder if we should be proud of being the first to escape or worried that we're the only people dumb enough to abandon the relative safety for a dark runway peppered with gunfire and the sounds of the dead.

It only takes a moment for my question to be answered. As Bishop and I crouch in the shadow of our cabin door a shape emerges into the light just a few yards away. It's a man.

Correction: it *was* a man, once.

Now... not so much. As the figure moves into the dim light it becomes obvious he's infected. He stands in a hospital gown, streaked with blood and trailing IV lines from both arms. He has about six inches on me, and his arms look almost as thick as my legs. There's no way I could take him down without a gun, and even if I had one I'd probably miss when this hulking monster came barreling towards us.

He turns quickly in the small pool of light, swinging his head back and forth as if he's sniffing the air for a target, and as he turns towards us and the light catches his face it's all I can do to keep myself from gasping. He's been mutilated almost beyond recognition. He drools from a gummy, toothless mouth, and his infected eye sockets weep with pus. It's hard to tell in the half light but it looks as if someone took a soldering iron to his eyeballs. The milky, misshapen, useless burst orbs stare out blindly towards us, almost as if he can still see us crouching in the darkness. *Did he do that to himself?*

He takes a step towards us, perhaps sensing our presence somehow. Beside me I feel Bishop tense to run, and I quickly grip his arm and squeeze as hard as I can. *No. Don't move.* I shake my head and point towards the guy's ruined eyes. I know he can't see us. If we just stay quiet and still we might be able to wait until—

A scream echoes from a cabin in the next row. In an instant the man breaks into a silent run straight towards it, ricocheting blindly off the wall of the cabin then tracing its sides with his hand, searching for a way in until he finally reaches the open door. The scream rings out again as someone inside tries far too late to pull it closed. All along the row I hear similar screams, ended by the groans of the infected. I start to run. I don't need to hear people die.

I run without thinking, just trying to get the fuck away from here in case there are more infected nearby. I break from the row of cabins, across the empty asphalt and out onto the wet, cool grass between the runway and the service roads leading back to the terminal; that strange, fallow no man's land you watch as you wait for your plane to taxi back to the gate, dotted with numbered markers that presumably mean something to the pilot.

My feet sink an inch or so in the soft, wet mud as I run, an odd sensation after walking for a month on the firm steel floor of the cabin. I feel like I'm stepping back on dry land after a long spell at sea, or like I'm stuck in one of those nightmares in which the air is as thick as molasses, and I'm struggling to flee while something terrifying draws closer and closer with each sucking step.

For a moment I panic as I sense a presence behind me. I hear movement and heavy breathing, and when I risk a quick glance behind I almost laugh out loud when I see the red faced Bishop struggling to keep up. In my panic I'd almost forgotten he was with me. I open my mouth to tell him to slow down for a moment, but before the first word escapes my mouth I trip on something solid, unseen in the darkness, and tumble forward and down a steep slope that suddenly appears before me.

I roll down the slippery slope, tumbling over a couple of times before I land hard, face first in something soft and moist. I try to raise myself up but my hands sink wrist deep in wet slurry. I feel like I'm sinking in it. Drowning. Being pulled down into black quicksand. I tug my hands from the grasping, sucking mud and scramble about for a grip on something solid, and after a moment my fingers meet something familiar but entirely unexpected. I probe around, confused.

A gaping mouth. Lips. Teeth. A chin covered in rough stubble.

I snatch my hand back in revulsion and clutch it against my chest, blindly checking for bite marks with my other hand. I open my eyes wide and try to adjust to the lack of light, but the pitch blackness seems even deeper down here, as if there's something blocking even the dim shapes of the clouds above. I'm blind.

I gingerly touch my hand to the ground beneath me again, and immediately realize what I'm touching. I know where I am. I know what they've done.

I scramble wildly out of the ditch, dragging myself up the wet, slippery slope using the short steel pole from the bed as a kind of ice pick, driving it into ground that feels far too firm to be soil. When I finally reach the lip of the slope and feel solid earth beneath my hands I find Bishop standing at the top, his lower lip quivering as he looks down at the dark shapes beneath him.

There's a roof of camouflaged netting held above the pit, suspended on stakes that surround it, holding it in place to hide it from view. Now the smell hits me fully. It's on my clothes, covering my hands and in my mouth. It's everywhere, and I know it's a stink that will take more than a shower to remove. It will live in my memory forever.

Hidden beneath the netting in the pitch darkness lie hundreds of bodies, all of them clad in the same blue hospital gowns as the infected man we saw at the cabin. A few of the bodies have been dumped towards the top of the slope, close to the edge of the netting where a little light can reach them. They're all the same. Puncture wounds in the arms from IV lines. Eyes poked out. Teeth yanked from their mouths.

"What the hell is this, Tom?" Bishop asks, his voice wobbling on the verge of tears. "What happened to them?"

"They were guinea pigs."

We both spin around at the sound of the voice behind us. In the darkness the figure is barely visible, kitted out in a dark green military uniform, her face blackened with grease paint.

"Who the fuck are you?" I demand, feeling stupid even as I raise the pipe in case I need to fight her off. She just tilts her head and swings her M16 down from her shoulder as if to say *just try it, asshole.*

"We came to save these sorry bastards," she says, looking down into the pit with disgust.

"Looks like we left it too late." She turns away from us and calls back over her shoulder. "Found it, Warren. You're not gonna like it."

Another figure emerges from the darkness in the direction of the runway, hidden from view by the distant glow of the floodlights behind him until he's almost on top of us. He's dressed the same as the woman, but he has a long rifle slung over his shoulder. As he reaches the pit he slows and stares at me and Bishop.

"Two guys. Seriously, two fucking guys made it?"

The woman nods. "Don't beat yourself up. We could have come two nights ago and rescued fifty, but it's just as likely we would have been shot at the door and hundreds more would have died. Besides, it's our fault. We should have guessed they'd have infected locked up in the same damned boxes."

Warren shakes his head and looks me up and down like he's judging a disappointing show dog. He snorts derisively and spits before turning away from the pit and setting off towards the terminal. As he turns away he mutters in disgust. "One of you guys better fucking cure cancer."

The pistol feels heavy in my hand. Heavier than I remember. It feels like I'm carrying a half brick, but I don't mind the weight. I'm just enjoying the feeling of safety it gives me, knowing that if something comes rushing towards me I won't have to wait until the last moment and hope I time the swing well enough to put it down with my short stick. I may not be a great shot, but at least now I'll have to chance to deal with a threat before I can feel its breath on my face.

"You ever fired one of those?" the woman asks, doubtfully.

"Yeah, of course," I reply, with a confidence that suggests I spend every weekend down at the range, then I reconsider. What's the point in trying to bullshit a soldier? "I mean, not for a long time. Just once, actually. I spent a day at an army base in Mongolia and they let me play around with a couple of their guns." I struggle to remember long-forgotten details. "I think the pistol I used was called a Makarov. Or is it Kamarov? And I tried a sniper rifle." I nod towards the guy, Warren.

"Though I guess you're all set for a sniper. I also drove a tank for a while."

She smiles and nods condescendingly. "Uh huh. OK, well I'll let you know if we need you to drive any tanks for us. In the meantime, keep the safety on and don't point that thing at anything you don't want dead. Understand? Good boy."

I nod, my cheeks hot with embarrassment. I never much cared that I wasn't a guy's guy before the last month. Shit, I was a journalist. I made my living with a pen and a laptop, and I only went into that game because I didn't want to do a real job. I long ago came to peace with the idea that I'd never set panties on fire with my masculinity, and it's only now I realize that I should have made at least a little effort to learn how to be useful now that words aren't needed any more. I feel like a third wheel for the whole world, like a telegraph operator working at Google.

"I'm Vee, by the way. Victoria Reyes. The guy with the bad attitude is Warren Campbell. You?"

"Tom. Freeman. And the big guy is Bishop."

She looks over at the lumbering giant walking ten steps away with a peaceful, vacant expression on his face. "First name? Last name?"

I shake my head. "Just Bishop. Trust me, don't ask."

She narrows her eyes curiously. "What do you mean, don't ask?"

"Seriously, you don't want to poke that hornet's nest. Just call him Bishop, OK?"

I can tell by the puzzled smile on her face that she won't drop it. She walks across my path until she's close enough to whisper. "Hey Bishop, what's this I hear about your name?"

Bishop spins on me with rage in his eyes and bellows. "Damn it, Tom, you promised you wouldn't tell anybody!"

"*Will you guys keep it the fuck down?*" hisses Warren, crouching behind the barrier at the side of the road, scanning around for signs of movement. "We're not out of the woods yet."

Vee whispers, trying to calm Bishop. "It's OK, it's OK, I was just kidding. Tom didn't tell me anything. It was just a joke."

Bishop clenches and unclenches his fists, looking between me and Vee as if he's trying to sense a lie. Eventually he relaxes. "OK, that's alright then. Just don't tell, OK? You promised not to tell."

I nod and whisper back. "Sure, buddy, I won't tell. It's OK." Vee walks back across me, and I drop my voice even lower. "I'll tell you later."

We continue in silence for the next ten minutes until we finally reach our getaway vehicle. I was expecting something like Sergeant Laurence's Stryker, or at least some kind of military Jeep, and I'm a little surprised when Warren stops beside a beat up old Toyota, pops the trunk and pulls out a soft carry case for his sniper rifle.

"Wow, I see we're riding in style."

Vee snorts. "It's got wheels, an engine and a tank full of gas. Good enough for us." She tugs open the rear door and nods at Bishop, who slides in before Warren follows him. "You're riding shotgun, cowboy. Warren needs to play with his wife for a while in the back."

Warren lets out a sarcastic laugh, settles himself in the rear seat and sets about stripping down his rifle. "You couldn't possibly understand the deep relationship a sniper forms with his rifle, you dumb grunt. Now get in and try not to crash."

I hop in the front passenger seat and take a look at my gun as Vee starts the engine and tears away onto the highway. I still don't really know what I'm looking at, but I see the words Pietro Beretta engraved in the side of the barrel. I've at least *heard* of Berettas, even though I don't know squat about guns. I squint to read the smaller letters beside the name of the gun, and a moment later I jerk forward as the car squeals to a halt.

"Gimme that!" Vee scolds, pulling the gun from my hands. "You had the fucking thing pointed right at my head. I told you, only ever point this at something you want to stop moving." She holds it up to the courtesy light and sees it's safe, then hands it back to me." Always assume it's loaded, and always assume the safety's off. I've been through too much shit to be taken out by friendly fire." She puts the car back in gear and pulls away. "Oh, and don't drop it. That belonged to my husband."

Despite my embarrassment I sense a certain tone in her voice. "Is he...?"

"He doesn't need it any more," she replies curtly, and I get the feeling it's a subject I wouldn't want to press. I fall silent and stare out the window at a world I haven't seen for a month. It all looks very different now.

We're heading south on a broad, empty highway. Almost empty, anyway. Every couple hundred meters by the side of the road lies a pile of wrecked cars that look like they were bulldozed out of the way. I vaguely remember seeing some abandoned vehicles on the road when we first arrived at the airport, so I guess the path was cleared when the base at the airport was expanded and resupplied.

The power's out now, as far as the eye can see. When I last passed this way it felt almost as if life was going on as usual. The streetlights were on, and businesses still appeared to be open on the roads that crossed beneath the highway. It almost felt like the world was normal beyond New York, and we'd escaped from nothing but a bad dream. Now it looks as if the nightmare followed us out. Every building looks abandoned, and a fair number of them have been burned out. I can't imagine that there could be anyone still alive down there, but—

"Hey, did you see that?" I ask, spinning around to Vee. "There was someone moving around down there!"

She doesn't even bother to look. "Yeah, wouldn't surprise me. There are still a few infected around here. A few looters. Maybe a few idiots who think this is a big scam so the government can take their property. They'll be dead soon enough if they're too dumb to leave."

"Jesus." I stare down at the roads as we fly by overhead, gawping in amazement at the desolation. I've got so many questions, I don't know where to begin. "OK, you gotta catch us up. We've been locked in a box for a month. What's going on?"

Vee tugs a pack of cigarettes from her pocket, pulls one out between her lips and offers the pack around. I grab one gratefully, accept her light and enjoy the first pull as I wait for her answer.

"Well," she says, taking her hands from the wheel to cup the flame as she lights hers, "we're fucked. Absolutely, positively screwed with our pants on."

Warren chuckles in the back seat. "Man, you guys'll wish you stayed in your little box. At least you got three square meals in there."

Vee frowns in the rear view mirror then looks back to the road. "You've been at the camp since this whole shitstorm started, yeah?" I nod. "So you know New York is toast?"

I nod again. "Bishop and I were there. We saw it up close. Only just got out alive."

"Oh man, what a sight that must have been." I notice she's got a faint smile on her face, but she wipes it off when she sees my scowl. "Sorry, I don't want to make light of it, but it must have been something else to watch it happen." She senses the mood and moves on. "Sorry. Anyway, couple hours later they gave D.C. the same treatment. We thought we'd caught it in time, wiped all of those motherfuckers out, but then we heard about the President."

She cracks open the window and taps out her ash. "When they decided to raze the capital Howard and the VP were down in the White House bunker. I don't know exactly what happened, but I guess they couldn't get to Andrews AFB. The whole city was such a clusterfuck there was no way they could get a motorcade through the streets without riding behind a tank, and they probably couldn't rendezvous with Marine One either. All I know for sure is that they tried to get out to the north by road just before the bombs fell.

"They didn't make it. Maybe the motorcade got caught in the tail end of the blast, who knows, but VP Lynch was definitely killed at the scene. As for the President... well, all they told us was that she was injured. They say she's been in a medically induced coma for the last month. I'm guessing she got bit, but they don't want to admit someone from her security team had to put down the President with a bullet. Whatever really happened, we know that most of the Secret Service detail was taken out by infected, and this was outside the blast zone. We don't know how many there are, but we know we didn't mop them all up like we planned. The infection has spread far beyond New York and D.C. Most of the military has been pulled back to guard the edge of the quarantine zone, and this whole chunk of the country is like the wild west. Anyway, after D.C. went dark they put that asshole Lassiter in charge."

"Lassiter?" I almost spit the name. "I hate that guy."

Vee forces out a bitter laugh. "Yeah, you didn't like him when he was just a religious nut who thought anyone who didn't go to his church deserved to burn in hell. You should see him now."

"Come on, how could he get any worse than he already was?" I laugh. Before the attacks the Speaker was already a political punchline. He was one of those guys who made wild, nonsense claims like women only got raped because they were being punished for their sins, and gays are responsible for stock market crashes. He was a lunatic who embarrassed moderate Republicans, and he only held onto his job because he had dirt on every politician who'd dared set foot in Washington for the last thirty years. Well, that and the fact that the Republicans never dared challenge him in the primaries, and his district hadn't come within twenty points of electing a Democrat since buckled hats were the height of style.

Warren looks up from his gun. "How could he get worse? Well, if we hadn't come save your ass tonight you would have been about 24 hours from finding out." He spits on the barrel and starts polishing it with a rag. "Lassiter was gonna have you killed."

Eight Days Earlier

Warren pushes his meal around the tray with a look of disgust, as if it could possibly taste any worse than the average meal he'd been eating every day since he enlisted. "This food is shit."

Vee looks up from her notebook. "Yeah, I think you mentioned that once or twice, Warren."

He drops his fork in the tray and puts it on the dash. "No, I mean *really* shit. Even worse than usual. Like... I don't know, I think it's off." He scoops up a forkful and holds it out. "Here, try it."

"I don't want to try your food, Warren."

"Just *try* it."

She snaps her notebook closed and glowers at him. "Warren, it's the end of the fucking world. Get used to bad food or go hang yourself with your belt. I don't really care which, but if you keep complaining I'm going to feed you that whole fucking tray."

Warren sulks at his fork. "Hey, I was just trying to make conversation."

"Well don't." She opens her book again and pretends to read the handwritten scrawl for a minute, painfully aware of Warren's downhearted look. "Sorry," she reluctantly mutters. "I'm just worried about Karl. He should have been back ten minutes ago."

Warren tosses his tray out the window and winds it back up, licking his fingers. "You got nothing to worry about, Vee. Karl could take down a rhino. He'll be fine."

Vee plays with her radio for a second, checking she's receiving properly. "If you loved anything other than that damned rifle you'd understand, Warren. You never stop worrying. Not for a single minute."

Warren gently pats the rifle wrapped in its soft case on his lap. "Yup, well I guess I'll never find out. Old Nadine would never let me take up with another woman." He smiles. "See, me and her? We have this bond you just don't get with regular love. We're always there for each other, come hell or high water. She's never let me down as long as she's been with me. That's real love, Vee. It's simpler than your human love. Beautifully uncomplicated." He strokes the case lovingly, and pauses for a moment. "I have to admit, though, as a relationship it's lacking a little in the sex department."

Vee laughs. "Come on, Warren. Don't try to tell me you've never—" Her thought is cut off by a hiss from the radio, followed by a voice.

"You've got infected incoming on your six, guys." Vee visibly relaxes at the sound of her husband's voice. "I'm coming in fast, and I wouldn't say no to a little backup. Over."

Vee grabs her M16 as Warren slips his rifle from its case, and within moments they're in position, Warren standing through the sunroof with his gun mounted on a bipod and Vee racing back along the sidewalk to find herself a solid firing position to cover Karl's approach.

He comes around the corner at a sprint, in one hand his Beretta and in the other a grenade, the pin pulled. Moments after he appears a flock of infected come racing after him, appearing around the corner in a closely packed group.

"Grenade, five o'clock, twenty yards," instructs Vee into her radio. She watches as Karl tosses it back and slightly to the right without looking. It lands just ahead of the pack and explodes as they pass over, sending three of them straight to the ground and leaving two more running at half speed, their legs damaged. Still seven more are in pursuit, at least until Vee and Warren open fire.

Warren takes out three in quick succession, calmly firing as if he's under no pressure at all, counting out his breaths and squeezing the trigger like he's playing a video game. Two head shots and one in the chest, a lucky shot that takes out the spinal cord on the way out.

Now the flock is down to four, and they enter Vee's firing range as Karl moves aside to give her a clear angle. She rests her elbow on the trunk of the car in front of her, carefully takes aim and squeezes off a few rounds from her M16. Three more infected go down one after the other as they're hit in rapid, controlled sprays.

Karl is just a couple of car lengths away now, with a single chaser remaining along with two more limping far behind. Warren takes out the two injured almost as an afterthought, while Vee allows Karl the pleasure of whipping around and taking out the final one, a skinny woman in a dirty pink t-shirt, with his Beretta. A single shot to the head is all it takes to put her on the ground.

Karl turns back to Vee and smiles, relieved. "If you guys didn't save me any of that shitty casserole there'll be hell to pay. I haven't eaten a thing since this morning. Hey Warren, can you fetch me some of that swill?"

Vee slings her gun over her shoulder and turns back towards the car just as a warning cry rings out from Warren. She turns back to Karl and watches in horror as the world slips into slow motion.

Karl's head shot wasn't accurate enough. It only grazed the woman, sending her to the ground without finishing her off. Even as Vee starts to swing her M16 back down she knows she can't move quickly enough. Karl's gun is already holstered at his hip, and Warren has begun to lower his rifle back into the car.

She catches Karl on his bare arm in mid-turn. It doesn't even look as if she's going for the bite. She just happens to catch him with her teeth as she lunges forward, and the infected will never pass up an opportunity. She bites down hard and tries to twist her neck to tear away a chunk of flesh.

Karl's closed fist comes down hard on her shoulder, sending her sprawling to the ground. A kick with a heavy boot spins her onto her back. He slides his Beretta from the holster and puts three shots between her eyes.

Vee can't speak. She can barely move. She didn't have a clear view but she only has to look at Karl's slumped shoulders to know what happened, and when he turns around and she sees his face her worst fears are confirmed.

He looks down at his bloodied arm. Pin pricks of blood blossom on the bite mark a couple of inches beneath his rolled up sleeve. Karl wipes them away, and moments later they appear again. It's only a tiny bite, barely more than a graze. It wouldn't even need stitches, but Vee knows that's not the point.

"We have orders," Karl mutters, tugging a crumpled envelope from his pants pocket. He sets it down on the asphalt in front of him, smiles at Vee and whispers, "I love you."

She doesn't try to stop him. They both know what needs to be done. They both made a pact back at the beginning, and she knows he's even more stubborn than her. *Never infected.* That was the deal. When the time came they'd die the right way, on their own terms. Clean. Quick.

She doesn't speak as he raises the Beretta to his mouth. She holds her closed fist over her heart and closes her eyes until she hears the shot, and doesn't open them again until she hears the body of her husband hit the ground.

She promised him she wouldn't cry.

It's a couple of hours before Vee manages to speak. She sits in silence in the driver's seat of the car as Warren takes watch through the sunroof, guarding the perimeter with his rifle. No infected come.

He almost wished they would. Maybe it would be a little easier if Vee had something to take out her anger on. Something she could beat with the butt of her gun until she stopped seeing Karl's face. Until she could stop thinking about his body bundled up in a tarp in the trunk of the car.

The sun is almost setting when Warren feels a tug on his leg. He looks down through the sunroof and sees Vee's red-rimmed eyes looking up at him, holding a blood stained sheet of paper in her hand.

"Our orders," she croaks, her voice dry and and scratchy. "We're just Lassiter's private army now." Her lip curls with hate. "That's what Karl died for."

Warren takes the paper from her loose grip, pulls it up and smooths it out on the roof of the car.

Supply of test subjects at Camp One critical. Round up any remaining residents of Zone Fourteen for delivery to Major Armitage. All constitutional rights suspended. Priority One.

It may have seemed fairly innocent had they not already heard the rumors about Camp One. They'd been circulating through the east coast ranks for a couple of weeks now, and while at first they'd sounded crazy it now seemed like they couldn't be anything but completely true.

Camp One had begun as a simple temporary refugee camp, a place where the survivors of New York could be housed while the military swept the outskirts of the city and ensured the outbreak had been contained. Vee herself had delivered survivors to the camp in the first few days. She'd felt proud with every truckload that she'd done her part to save the lives of innocents.

Then the news of Lassiter's accession broke, and the orders began to change. The military proper was pulled out of the camp, replaced by a few high ranking officials supported by private security forces. Vee received orders to accompany a resupply convoy that seemed more suited to a prison or a biotech lab than a refugee camp. Hundreds of secure prefab cells outfitted with electromagnetic locks. Medical equipment that seemed designed more for experimentation than for treating the wounded. Shackles. Secure beds. Absurd volumes of anesthesia

Outside the camp the tone of the orders began to change. In the beginning their orders were simply to assist survivors and to help them reach the camp if they didn't feel safe in their homes. Now the orders became more explicit, and much more worrying. They were ordered to compel survivors to the camp. They were even issued tranquilizer guns, and authorized to use them against anyone unwilling to go voluntarily.

The numbers kept adding up. In the first two weeks following the attacks Vee personally delivered several hundred civilians to Camp One, and she knew her truck had been just one of dozens working in the area. Thousands were delivered, and none had ever been seen to leave. The rumors shifted and morphed like a game of Telephone, but when a guard finally contacted a friend outside the camp the truth became clear.

Lassiter was trying to weaponize the contagion. He wasn't trying to cure it. Wasn't trying to find a vaccine. He was simply trying to find a way to use the infection for his own purposes.

And he was using civilians as test subjects.

He'd always seemed like the kind of guy who'd want to ride alongside the four horsemen of the apocalypse. Even before the attacks it had been an open secret in Washington that Lassiter was a religious zealot of the worst kind, a man who'd spent his life just waiting for the opportunity to score a decisive victory over his enemies. He was the sort of guy who believed - *truly* believed, with every ounce of his being - that he was God's messenger. It was a poisonous belief that excused any amount of evil carried out in his name.

He'd been dug into the capital ecosystem like a tick for decades, but both his allies and opponents had always managed to find ways to keep anything really dangerous far from his desk, in the same way that Supreme Court Justices delay the important decisions when it looks like one of their number might have started on the long road towards senility. He just couldn't be trusted.

And now there was nobody left to hold him back. He'd found himself at the top of the pile, and everybody who knew him - hell, anybody who even had the slightest interest in politics - knew what that meant. It meant he was free to be the dictator he'd always dreamed of becoming.

Warren reads the order a second time, then a third. He lifts his rifle from the roof and slips down to the front passenger seat. Vee still stares out the front window at something that isn't there, and never will be again.

"What do you wanna do?" he asks quietly. He's already decided to follow Vee's lead. He trusts her with his life, and she's already proved she's good for it many times over. Whatever she decides will be the right call.

She stays silent for a long moment, turning her head from the window down to the bloody paper in his hands.

"Did I ever tell you how Karl and I met?" she asks, almost in a whisper.

Warren shakes his head. "No, I don't think so."

She smiles as she remembers. "We were stationed together in Zeraa, a nothin' little smudge on the map about twenty clicks south of Aleppo. This was a couple of years ago, right at the start of the ground assaults. Not sure if you were on active duty back then.

"We had intel that ISIL were transporting chemical weapons along the back roads to try to take back the city. Really nasty shit. The intel seemed pretty solid. Enough to authorize a strike, anyhow, but I wasn't so sure. Something about it just didn't feel right to me, but it wasn't my call. I could make a recommendation but... well, you know how that shit works." She lights a cigarette and take a long, slow drag. "Karl was my new CO, just arrived that week. He had his orders and I had mine, but I argued with him. Flat out refused to lead the strike. He could have had me court-martialled, but instead he reported that an equipment failure on one of the support drones forced a delay.

"Turns out it was a wedding party. Ground forces stopped the motorcade and checked the vehicles before they reached the city. There were fourteen kids. Two pregnant women. About a dozen elderly people, and they weren't carrying so much as a peashooter between them." She flicks the ash from her cigarette and takes a drag, making the embers glow bright red.

"I disobeyed the first order he ever gave me. I'll disobey the last." She takes the paper from Warren's hand and holds the cigarette to it until the flame catches. "He wouldn't want this. He wouldn't want us helping some lunatic President spread this shit to his enemies. That's not the country he signed up to serve. That's not the country I want this to become.

"Now, Warren, you can come with me or I can drop you off close to the base. It's up to you, but if you come with me I need you to know something." She winds down the window and tosses out the burning paper, throwing her cigarette after it.

"I intend to misbehave."

I listen in rapt attention as Vee tells the story, chain smoking with one eye on the road and the other looking out for infected.

"Wow," I say, looking down at the gun in my hand and suddenly understanding why Vee was so precious about it. "So you guys deserted."

She shrugs her shoulders and blows out a plume of smoke. "If that's the way you want to look at it, sure. I don't see it that way."

Warren pipes up from the back of the car. "You have to ask yourself who you really serve. Is it your immediate superior? The President? I don't think it's either. Call me naive, but when I signed up it was to serve my country, not just one man on a power trip. I happily signed on the dotted line and agreed to give my life for the United States. I never agreed to go to war against my own people. None of us did."

Vee nods. "He's right. The way I see it the real deserters are those who stayed. They've abandoned the people they promised to protect, and now they're just following orders." Another drag on the cigarette. Another angry plume of smoke. "It's not like we haven't seen this shit before. My grandpa had to go to Europe to fight a bunch of guys who were just following orders."

I can't argue, but I don't know what to say. I just nod, stay silent, and light another cigarette.

"Edgar was there."

I turn in my seat and see Bishop shifting in his seat. I thought he'd been sleeping, but it seems he was just listening with his eyes closed.

"How do you mean?" I ask.

"Edgar." Bishop repeats. "He was in one of those, umm, camps in Europe. Remember?"

I'd almost forgotten about that. Before he died Edgar had told us the story. I'd only been half listening at the time, since I really didn't want to hear shit like that considering our situation, but he'd told us he came from a little town just outside Kraków, Poland. He was just a baby when the German occupation began, and his first memories were of life in the Kraków ghetto. Sometime around 1942 he'd been moved to Plaszow, then two years later transferred to Flossenburg in Bavaria. By the time the camp was liberated in '45 he was ten years old, his family was gone, and the only things he owned were the threadbare clothes on his back.

"Edgar was our friend," Bishop rumbles, his voice filled with anger. "They hit him in the face with a gun and killed him. They didn't have to do that. He just didn't want to be locked up any more."

Vee turns to me with fire in her eyes. "Doesn't that make you mad? Doesn't it make you want to just reach down their throats and tear out their lungs?"

I nod. "Of course it does. I'm fucking furious, but what can we do? The camp's gone. Everyone's dead."

From the back seat I hear a dull click as Warren slots ammo into his magazine. "No. Hardly any of them are. We only got the guys who guarded the prison. The fuckers who built the place are still out there, probably already planning another. So, first priority," he says, "we find somewhere to sleep, and you can learn how to use that gun you're holding so I don't have to carry your ass across the country. Then we can get you and the big guy to Columbus, and we can blow the fucking lid on what Lassiter's been doing."

"Columbus? What's in Columbus?"

Vee chimes in. "Columbus is the first decent sized city outside the quarantine zone. Most of the big cities have been evacuated, but there's still some media working out of Columbus. Couple of radio stations and what's left of the big New York and D.C. papers set up there after the attacks. We have to at least try. If I know Lassiter he won't give up after just one little setback. He'll set up another camp, then another, then another. He'll kill as many people as it takes to win his insane war, and we owe it all the people in that fucking mass grave to give people a chance to fight back." She maneuvers the car around a pile of wrecks and guns the engine. "So, are you coming along for the ride?"

I look back at Bishop, who nods furiously. "Well, I guess somebody has to take keep old Lennie here out of trouble. I'm in."

"Lennie?" Vee asks. "That's Bishop's name?"

I shake my head. "No, that's not— it's a joke. *Of Mice and Men*? George and Lennie? Alfalfa? Rabbits? Ringing any bells?" I'm met by blank faces all round. "Not a book crowd, huh? OK, fuck it. Let's go take down a President."

Terrence Lassiter emerges from the chapel with an expression of profound calm, in stark contrast to the vein-popping rage he'd felt as he walked in. His visits to the chapel were always invigorating. Even after weeks without feeling the warmth of the sun through the windows of his own church, and even though he hadn't seen his dear family since he'd left the surface, no matter how troubled he felt as he entered he always emerged from his private sanctuary at peace, his resolve renewed.

He'd be the first to admit that the last month had been... trying, to say the least. The vast expansion of his responsibilities had been almost overwhelming, but it was a challenge he'd faced several times before. The first was when he felt the calling to become a minister as a much younger man. Overnight his flock expanded from four - his wife and darling children - to many hundreds. Then, just a few short years later, he'd been called on once again to represent the first congressional district of Arkansas and once more his flock grew, that time to hundreds of thousands.

His promotion to Speaker at the age of 67 was even greater, and he saw it as a chance to speak to an even larger congregation. Not just to the men and women who served with him in the House but to each and every one of the millions of American citizens they represented. After three years in the position he'd assumed it was God's intention that he rise no further. That this would be where he could serve his Lord best.

He'd been wrong. Oh, how he'd underestimated the will of the Lord. He'd never imagined He would bless him with yet more bounty, nor demand of him an even greater sacrifice, but Terrence Lassiter knew in his heart that he was equal to the challenge. He knew he could answer the call, just as he always had before.

He'd never presume to understand God's ineffable motivations, of course, but in moments of quiet reflection over the last few weeks he often wondered if he'd not been cast in the role of Gideon from the Book of Judges. Gideon's tale had always been one of his favorite Old Testament stories, and it had always been a crowd pleaser when he preached it before his congregation.

Gideon was tasked by the Lord to free the Israelites, who had turned away from Yahweh and chosen to worship false gods, from a Midianite army 135,000 men strong. To serve His will Gideon amassed his own army of 32,000, but the Lord said they were too many. With so many men the Israelites might claim that they had been saved not by the Lord but simply by a mighty army, so God instructed Gideon to send all who wished to leave home. 22,000 left, and 10,000 remained.

Still God said this was too many. How could the Israelites be certain that it was God's will that they be saved from the Midianites? Still they may claim it was only Gideon's army that had freed them.

Gideon, eager to bring glory upon God, winnowed down his forces yet further until only 300 remained. He was afraid that such a small force may not triumph against the Midianite hordes, but he put his trust in the Lord. God, always true to his word, allowed those 300 a great victory, freeing the Israelites from their siege.

Lassiter had considered this story many times since he'd found himself thrust into the Presidency, and each time he felt closer and closer to understanding God's wishes for him. Like Gideon, Lassiter had begun with a mighty army. On his first day in office he'd controlled the massed forces of the entire United States military, the greatest fighting force in the history of the planet, and surely the equal to any earthly foe.

God, in his boundless wisdom, had decided that a victory using such awesome power would be insufficient to convince his deniers - not just the Israelites this time, but the many millions of deviants, blasphemers and followers of false prophets around the world, all of whom who failed to recognize the supremacy of God.

And so He saw fit to weaken the forces at Lassiter's command so as to better display that the victory, when it came, would be God's will. First came the loss of Roberts, the Secretary of Defense, who refused to understand the obvious need to research the infection that had overrun the United States. His resolve was weak, and Lassiter had no choice but to banish him to the surface above Site R. Perhaps if he chose to turn to God he may be allowed to live, and Lassiter would be among the first to offer him forgiveness.

With Roberts' departure it seemed prudent to put direct operational control of the military back into the hands of the Joint Chiefs of Staff, men who had spent a lifetime following orders, and who truly understood that painful sacrifices must sometimes be made for the greater good. He assumed they'd understand the need to carry out vital research at Camp One; that the loss of a few thousand test subjects was more than outweighed by the ability to wield such influence over the wider world. Like Roberts, however, these men lacked the necessary resolve, and saw fit to resign their commissions rather than carry out their Commander in Chief's orders. They too were banished to the surface.

More resignations came, and then more, until eventually Lassiter saw that simple banishment was impractical. The civilian traitors were confined to the holding cells of the complex, while the military commanders were justly executed to pay for their treachery.

Finally the bleeding began to stop. When his remaining staff understood the harsh consequences of disloyalty he was pleased to see how quickly they fell in line. Lassiter felt terrible for instilling in them such fear and he'd asked for guidance and forgiveness during many of his visits to the chapel, but he knew that - in time - the men and women working under him would understand that he had been correct, and that they were working towards a righteous cause.

Now, as Lassiter steps through the door of the situation room hidden a hundred meters beneath the surface of Raven Rock Mountain, he reflects that perhaps the Lord may finally consider his forces small enough to score a decisively righteous victory. Without the aid of the Secretary of Defense and the Joint Chiefs his command of the military is greatly weakened, with only a loyal few remaining to carry out his orders. The traitors have followed in the footsteps of Gideon's 22,000, returning home and forcing the Air Force and the Navy to stand down and reject all orders from his office. Much of the Army remains overseas, effectively stranded and unable to help the nation in its hour of need.

If Lassiter's faith wasn't quite so strong he might consider himself forsaken by his Lord, but - like the angel who appeared to Gideon and assured him that he was carrying out God's work - just as so many were abandoning him an unlikely ally arose to stiffen the President's resolve: Samuel Whelan, the Director of the Central Intelligence Agency.

It was Whelan who found the solution to Lassiter's military crisis, drawing on the vast network of covert operatives that were his pre-war stock in trade. It was he who suggested that the President extend certain promises to those operatives to ensure their loyalty. Promises of cash, of tracts of land in the quarantine zone and, for those military commanders who had remained loyal, a promise of promotion to political office once the crisis was over, to fill the many seats vacated by the cowards and traitors who had fled.

It was Whelan who helped Lassiter realize that the loss of the eastern states presented a tremendous opportunity. That far from a disaster the infection had simply wiped the slate clean on a country that had moved too far from God.

Whelan had been his savior. The President was under no illusions that the crafty, scheming old spymaster was a righteous man and he knew that once this crisis was over he'd need to be justly dealt with, but for now he made a useful if unlikely ally. With his help Lassiter would remake the United States in God's image, and it would be truly glorious.

"Mr. President, there's a problem."

Lassiter's chest swells for a moment at the sound of the term of office, just as it has each time he's heard it over the last month. He allows himself a brief moment of pleasure, then adds it to the long list of sins he'll need to ask forgiveness for on his next visit to the chapel.

"What is it now, Mr, Whelan?" He takes a seat at the end of the long table, several seats from Whelan, and bristles inwardly at the fact that the Director failed to stand with the proper respect as he entered the room. That infraction is added to the bottom of a very different, much longer list.

Whelan turns to the wall-mounted screen, a map of the United States, and presses a button on the intercom. "Can you show me grid seven?" The map immediately zooms in from the overview until the northeast fills the screen, narrows down until Lassiter recognizes New York, then zooms further until he sees the outline of Newark Airport.

"About an hour ago we lost contact with Camp One. Major Armitage failed to make his scheduled check-in, so we repositioned the satellite to see if we could get an idea of what was going on. This is Camp One at 10PM, and this," he presses a key on his console, and the image immediately switches, "is Camp One on the last pass about twenty minutes ago. You're looking at an infrared image to see past the cloud cover."

"Oh, good grief," sighs Lassiter, sinking into his seat. On screen a false color image appears to show a thick column of smoke extending north from the airport, while a dull red spot at the south end of the runway shows the residual heat from what looks like an explosion. "What do we think happened? An attack? An accident?"

Whelan chews his pencil for a moment before answering. "It was an attack. And not by infected, either. We've just received word from a unit sent to investigate that several guards were found dead at the scene. Sniper and small arms fire. And it looks like they took out the generators on site using military grade explosives."

"Traitors," curses Lassiter. "They'll be the death of us. Any casualties?"

Whelan steels himself for the outburst of rage he knows to expect. "Yes, sir. I'm sorry to say our losses were total. It seems the explosion disabled the locks on the holding cells, and a number of infected were released along with the remaining test subjects. The camp was overrun."

Lassiter stares at the screen for a moment, as if trying to pick out the attackers in the image. Whelan remains silent, waiting for the President to lash out at him as if this was his fault, but the usual attack doesn't come. Instead Lassiter simply removes his glasses, kneads the bridge of his nose with his fingers and looks back at Whelan.

"Are your teams in position?"

"Yes, sir."

"And they have the required stockpiles?"

Whelan ponders the question for a moment. "It'll be touch and go. We could use a few weeks to synthesize more, but... yes, I believe they may have enough, Mr. President."

Lassiter stands, pushing back his chair. "We go today. No more waiting. Understood?"

Whelan lifts the phone in front of him to connect to his field control unit. "Yes, I understand, sir. Umm, you have to give the order. I'm sorry, it's just a formality."

"Operation Crop Dust, Mr Whelan. I'm giving you the go order. Make it happen."

At that the President replaces his glasses, turns on his heel and strolls out of the room as if he and Whelan have just enjoyed nothing but a casual conversation. Nobody who didn't understand how Lassiter's mind worked would ever guess that he'd just casually ordered the largest and most ambitious air strike in the history of the human race.

Vee rubs her eyes and stifles a yawn, stretching her arms to loosen her tight muscles. "You don't need to sleep?" she asks.

I shake my head and push the magazine into its slot until I feel it click. "Nah. I've been sleeping for a month. I don't know how you guys sleep out here, anyway. Aren't you worried we'll be attacked?"

Vee shakes her head. "Nah, not so much. We're usually pretty safe a few floors up, so long as we don't attract attention. Most of them can't climb stairs so well now they've started to, you know, dry out and stuff. Honestly, they're not much of a danger unless they're fresh or they've eaten recently. Besides, it's a cost benefit analysis thing. We don't sleep tonight, we make a dumb mistake and get ourselves killed tomorrow. You gotta weigh up the risks."

I lift myself awkwardly from the carpeted floor and find my way in the darkness over to the window. It's too dark outside to see much from up on the fourth floor of this abandoned office building on the outskirts of a small town off Highway 78, but down at street level I'm sure I can see a couple of shapes moving slowly in the shadows. "What *are* they?"

"How do you mean?"

"I mean what makes them tick? Why do they try to kill?"

Vee gives me a surprised look. "Shit, you don't know? Man, you really have been stuck in a box, haven't you?" She reaches in her duffel bag and tugs out a couple of candy bars. "Here, eat something, you need the sugar," she says, tossing me a Milky Way.

"It's a fungus," she explains, tearing open her wrapper. "*Cordyceps bangkokii*, they call it. You ever heard of *Cordyceps*?"

I shake my head as I happily chew. I'd almost forgotten what chocolate tastes like.

"First couple of weeks the news talked about nothing else. I think I could probably teach a damned course on it by now." She chuckles and tosses her candy wrapper to the floor. "There's a species of fungus called...

umm, *Ophiocordyceps unilateralis*. It's found in the tropical forests of Thailand and Brazil, I think. I once saw a piece on it in an old David Attenborough nature documentary, and even back then I though this shit was creepy as hell. I don't know exactly how it works, but it's a type of fungus that attacks carpenter ants, and turns them into some kind of... well, I guess you could call them zombies. They just lose control. The *Cordyceps* compels them to climb the nearest tree, find a leaf and clamp on hard with their mandibles, then this shit starts to multiply inside them. After a few days the ants die and the fungus breaks through their exoskeleton and grows a long, gross tube that releases spores that drift down to the ground and land on more ants, and the whole disgusting process starts again. Circle of life, right?" She shivers with revulsion.

   "Anyway, some genius must have heard about this stuff and decided it'd be a great idea to see if they could tweak it enough that it infects humans. I don't know who it was, and I *really* don't know why they decided to do something so obviously dumb, but it looks like they succeeded. Shit, they didn't just succeed. They made this stuff even worse. *Cordyceps bangkokii* is just something else. Whoever played around with it knew exactly what they were doing. It's a near perfect organism, as long as your goal is to fuck up everyone's day.

"All it takes is a single spore in your blood. A scratch. A bite. A fleck of spit in your eye. That's all you need. Once it's inside you it feeds on your blood and multiplies faster than you can believe. I'm talking from one to billions in a matter of minutes, like your blood is a fucking all you can eat buffet. The spores follow your bloodstream up to your brain, and that's where the fun really begins. They just turn everything to mush. All your higher functions. Your thoughts, your memories, everything that makes you *you*, all gone. The only thing it leaves is the brain stem and just enough little bits of gray matter to keep you on your feet and moving."

She reaches for her cigarettes, taps one out of the pack and plays with it for a moment before lighting it. "Once the fungus has control its only goal is to make you pass it on to the next host. It keeps you alive like a life support machine. You're still breathing. Your heart's still beating, though it doesn't matter to the fungus if you're technically alive or dead. As long as your central nervous system is still working it can just guide you around like a meat puppet.

"Far as I can tell, the only thing these things feel is rage and hunger. They caught a few of them back in the first week before everything really went to shit, and they ran some tests on them. Turns out they've got about fifty times as much adrenaline rushing through them as an average person. They're permanently locked in fight or flight mode, and they always choose fight."

I look down at the street again, and suddenly it looks even more forbidding down there. The shapes lurking in the dark are just vehicles, mindless creatures compelled with every fiber of their being to chase us down and pass on the infection. They were already terrifying but now, somehow, they seem even more so. We're not just fighting individuals, but a force of nature itself.

How can we possibly beat nature?

"Earlier you said they've started to dry out. What did you mean?"

Vee lets out a chuckle. "Ah, now that's where we have the upper hand. This *Cordyceps* shit is clever, but it ain't perfect. I've been chasing these things down for a month now and I've yet to see a single one of them take a drink. I don't know for sure, but I think it destroys whatever part of the brain is responsible for basic self preservation. I guess they can't tell when they're thirsty any more, so they just don't drink until they die of dehydration."

"Huh, kinda like dolphins," I say.

Vee gives me a confused look. "You're gonna have to expand on that, Tom. Dolphins?"

"Yeah. See, dolphins can't survive on sea water. It'd kill them just like it'd kill us, so they draw all the water they need from the food they eat. In the wild that works out fine. It's just the way they evolved, so they don't know any different. The problem is that when they're in captivity they'll happily drink fresh water if they can get access to it, but then they won't eat for a week. So long as nobody notices they'll just keep happily drinking water until they eventually starve to death. They don't know the difference between thirst and hunger. Their brains just aren't wired up for it."

Vee nods. "Yeah, OK, that kinda makes sense. So if the fungus has destroyed the part of the brain that tells us when we're thirsty—"

"— the hypothalamus," I interrupt, happy that there's finally something I know about this fucked up situation that Vee doesn't.

"Right, the hypo... whatever. If that's gone these guys will just keep eating and won't bother to drink, and as long as they can't get the fluid they need from human flesh they'll eventually just die out."

"That sounds about right." I think back to something Vee said a moment ago. "Then again, you said the infected have a shitload of adrenaline running through them. The hypothalamus is responsible for regulating the adrenal glands, so maybe *Cordyceps* doesn't destroy it but just repurposes it. You know, turns that whole section of the brain into a loudhailer to yell at the adrenal glands to produce more and more. I'm just guessing. I'm not a scientist."

"You might be right," agrees Vee, lifting herself up with a grunt and joining me at the window. She looks down at the shapes moving beneath with a grimace. "I guess it doesn't really matter what's going on in their heads. As long as they're not getting enough water from their food they're living on borrowed time. We just have to wait them out. Just get through it one day at a time, and wait for the very last one of those fuckers to dry up and keel over. Then we take back the country and bury Lassiter beneath the pile of the corpses he made."

"You really think it'll be that simple? Do you really believe we can survive this?"

She nods. "We've survived this long. So long as we can stop more people getting infected I don't see why we can't get through it. Shit, you and Bishop got out of New York, right? If you can live through that you're pretty much invincible." She turns to me and lowers her voice. "Hey, that reminds me. You promised to tell me about Bishop's name. What's the big deal?"

I glance towards the door and lower my voice. "OK, I'll tell you, but you have to promise not to let him know. He's crazy sensitive about it. It's not a big deal, but you know how people can be weird about things like that." I try to keep the smile from my face. He's called Forrest."

Vee grins. "Like—"

"Yeah, like Gump. And he's a slow, friendly guy from Alabama. You can guess what it was like growing up."

"Jesus, poor guy." She falls silent for a moment, then grins again. "Damn, I really hope we won't need to run from any infected tomorrow. I don't think I could keep myself from yelling... well, y'know."

I try to stifle a laugh as Warren rushes through the door, breathing heavily, holding his wind up lamp back away from the door so it doesn't shine out through the window. "Hey, guys. I think you need to come and listen to the radio." I stop laughing as soon as I see his expression. "I think something's happening in Columbus."

The pilot grins broadly as he sees the lights of the city appear on the horizon through his windshield. He's been grinning constantly since the call came through two hours ago, and to be honest his lips are starting to ache a little now, but he just can't help himself. This is far and away the biggest night of his life. This is the night he becomes a hero, not only to Mandy and the kids but to every man, woman and child in Columbus.

Tonight the name Eric Peterson will go down in history. He may only be a small, insignificant cog in the great nation saving machine, but tonight his name will join those of a thousand other brave pilots who selflessly signed up for the President's volunteer air corps; brave pilots who are right now flying towards their own cities all across the country, all of them carrying a precious cargo.

Eric feels almost dizzy with pride. He can already imagine the hero's welcome awaiting him back at the airfield. He can imagine never having to pay for a drink again in the local bars, and being showered with praise by the assholes who used to mock him. He can imagine a tasteful marble monument, somewhere prominent in the rebuilt capital, with his name engraved on it; something he can show the grandkids one day. *See, kids, grandpa really was a hero in the war. He wasn't just the drunk idiot everyone thought he was.*

He can *definitely* imagine the welcome he'll receive when he gets home. For once, maybe, Mandy will look at him with pride rather than shame. For once she might be thinking of *him* when they make love. That'd make a nice change. Hell, maybe he'll get a little attention from some of the young girls at the bar, the ones who lean suggestively over the pool table and walk around in knotted shirts that show off their flat bellies. He wouldn't *do* anything with them, of course. It'd just be nice to know the option's there.

No. Scratch that last part. He'll need to set an example for the kids. Leering at young women doesn't fit with the heroic image racing through his head.

Eric Peterson, a humble, salt of the earth Ohio crop duster who did his part to save his country from annihilation. A man who stood up to be counted when the going got tough. A skilled pilot who dared all to save the lives of the hundreds of thousands cowering fearfully below.

Eric Peterson, *American Hero*.

Yeah. It has a nice ring to it.

He grips the stick of his trusty old American made Piper Pawnee, throttles down and drops his altitude slowly towards the 200 foot target. It'll be a challenging dump so close to the deck, maneuvering between the thirty or so buildings in the city that top that height, but he knows he's a capable pilot. He's confident he can glide safely between the skyscrapers for the three passes it'll take to cover the center of the city.

The sprawling suburbs of Columbus pass beneath him as he approaches. Somewhere down there Mandy has tucked the kids in bed and settled down to watch her shows. She doesn't know he's up here. He didn't have time to call her before he was pulled from the bar, bundled into a black SUV and whisked to the hangar. She probably thinks he's still getting hammered at McCluskey's with the guys right now. She's probably cursing his name, but she'll change her tune when she hears what he's done. When he walks in, sober and clear eyed, and tells her he's saved the city.

Here it is. He sees the narrow ribbon of the 270 pass beneath him, and he tugs the red tank release lever beside the stick. He can't see the fine mist spray from the ass of the plane, but he can hear the hydraulics whir as the nozzle opens. He can feel the upward pressure tugging at the stick as the scrappy little Piper lightens its heavy load.

He skirts the city center, pulls east towards Bexley and Whitehall then curves back around in a lazy arc, bringing it in for another pass, another spray. Out towards Valleyview and Upper Arlington then back once more. All those fancy houses he could never hope to afford. All those city folk who looked down their noses at him and wrote him off as a dumb hick. They'll all owe him their lives come the morning. Everyone will know his name.

He's flying so low he can see the people down in the streets below clear as day as they emerge from their homes and lean out their windows to see what's causing the racket above. They're probably cursing him right now. They have to get up for work in a few hours, and Eric's engines just woke the kids and set off the dog. A few of them are probably even calling the airfield to complain about the nuisance. Come the morning they'll be singing a different tune.

Would a ticker tape parade be asking too much? He doesn't know if they even do those any more, but it'd be real nice to sit in the back of a convertible, riding slowly through the city as thousands of people chant his name.

It takes a half hour of dusting before the tank runs almost dry. The gauge has been busted a few years, but he cuts it off when it feels like he has maybe five percent left. That should be more than enough.

This next part of the job is kind of off script, but he has one final special delivery to make before returning to the airfield. He guides the little Piper southwest out of the city back towards Bolton Field, but angles it so it'll take him just a couple of miles to the west. The lights begin to fade out here in the boondocks, but he doesn't need much light to find this particular target. He knows this place like the back of his hand. He could find it with his eyes closed.

There it is, a mile or so west of the cookie cutter suburban sprawl of New Rome. The unlit, unpaved track cuts a clear path between the overgrown fields and there, half hidden in a grove of willow trees at the very end of the trail, he spots the dirty white roof of his small home. The rusted wreck of an old pickup out front in a mass of crabgrass. The tire swing he put in for Dan rocking back and forth in the breeze. Out front the porch light is on, and he can almost imagine Mandy sitting out there watching her little portable set while she waits for him to return home.

Once again Eric drops to the deck, bringing his little plane down so low he almost grazes the treetops, and with a broad smile he tugs the red lever as he passes over, emptying the last of the tank directly above his wife and three sleeping children.

They'll be so proud of him. They'll be so proud of their old man when they wake up in the morning.

They'll be so, *so* proud to learn he saved the very last drops of vaccine for them.

The radio crackles as Warren adjusts the dial, searching back and forth in the dim light glowing from his lamp until he finally regains the signal.

"—see them from the window of our technician's booth. We have her out there right now checking out street level, but I can't actually get visual confirmation myself without leaving the studio. Kathy? Kathy, are you still with us, hon?"

Quick, shallow breathing emits from the speakers before the DJ returns. He speaks with the same clipped, affected radio newscaster voice everyone seems to use, but it does little to hide his panic. It takes me a few seconds to realize it's Barry Brooks - the Big Double Bee - a nationwide drive time DJ I've listened to for years. It seems strange to hear him talk about something serious, since his usual fare tends to lean towards wacky politics and celebrity gossip.

"OK, I don't seem to have Kathy right now, but I can only assume she's still in the building. I'll get an update for you just as soon as she returns to her booth but for now, to recap for listeners just tuning in, all I can say is that something troubling appears to be going on in the streets below our studio up on the twelfth floor of the LeVeque Tower on Broad Street. We... ah, we don't want to alarm listeners unduly so I really don't want to speculate on what exactly is the cause of the unrest, but I can tell you that there have been ongoing protests concerning the influx of refugees into the state in recent weeks that have threatened to spill over into violence. Obviously I don't want to make light of this... ah, or in any way diminish or dismiss the complaints of the protesters, but I'm sure all our listeners are with me in hoping that the unrest on the streets below is a simple protest and not... ah, OK, we have a caller on the line. I don't have Kathy to route the calls but I'm gonna try to put it on air. Caller, can you hear me?"

The voice comes through muffled and muddy, but audible. "Yeah I can hear you, Barry. Am I on?" It's a woman. She sounds terrified.

"You're coming through loud and clear, caller. Now, can you tell us where you are? Is anything going on in your location?"

"Barry, yeah, I'm just across the river from you in Franklinton about six blocks from the science museum. I'm real scared, Barry. I don't know what to do."

Barry lowers his voice to a comforting tone. "You're perfectly safe, caller, we're all right here with you. Now why don't you tell me your name, and try to tell me a little about what's happening on your side of the river?"

She sniffs. "It's Pam," she says, tears in her voice. "I was just, umm, I was about to get ready for bed about a half hour ago but then I heard a loud noise outside, like an engine or something, you know? So I went outside to try to figure out what was making all that racket and I saw a plane fly overhead. Real low, you know, like *too* low? It was headed over in your direction, and for a minute I just thought, *oh my gosh*, it's gonna hit one of the buildings, but it just went between them and then headed back out of town. But when it passed over the river I saw that it was... I don't know, *venting* something? There was something white coming out the back of the plane and drifting towards the ground, and just a few minutes later I started to hear screams out in the street. I was about to go look when I switched on the radio and heard you talking about some trouble."

Barry's voice is full of concern now. "Pam, are you somewhere safe? Don't go out to the street, Pam. Right now we just don't know what's happening, but I don't want you risking your safety out there. Are you safe, Pam?"

"Yeah, I'm in the upstairs bathroom right now, Barry, but I have to go fetch my daughter from her room. I'm gonna try to take a quick look out the window while I'm— oh honey, thank God. Come on inside, honey. Come on, it's safe in here. My gosh, you're burning up!"

"Pam, what's going on there? Talk to me, Pam."

A few loud clicks and muffled thumps come through the speaker, as if Pam set the phone down on the floor. After a moment her voice returns, more distant now. "Oh, honey, you've soaked right through your nightgown. It's OK, don't worry about it. Come on, come to momma. There's a good girl... No, honey, that's too hard. No. Stop it, honey. Stop it! Honey, *stop*..."

"Pam? Talk to me, Pam. What's happening?"

It sounds like the phone skates across the floor before a loud bang, maybe the sound of it hitting the wall, but the background noise is barely audible over the scream. It's ear splitting, and a long moment passes before Barry manages to cut off the call.

"Oh God, I'm sorry, listeners, I couldn't... I didn't know how to, ah..." Barry falls silent for a moment before continuing. "OK, I'm gonna see if I can figure out how to go mobile. I need to see what's going on in the street. Bear with me a second, I'm just... Look, if you're listening right now I'm begging you not to leave your homes. Just... just lock all your doors and windows and get to the most secure room in your house. Obviously we don't really know what's happening, but if this is airborne we're... just stay indoors and wait for help, OK?"

The sound cuts out for about twenty seconds. Dead air, not even static, then it suddenly returns with a confused jumble of echoing sounds.

"I don't know if I'm still on the air. I think I've got this rig wired up right, but I'm no technician. If you can still hear me I've just left the studio on the twelfth floor, and I'm headed to the windows overlooking Broad Street. I'm, ah... it's pretty dark in here, but I think I can make it across. OK, I'm here in the office of, ah... I think this is the Daystar broadcast studio. Here's the window..."

He falls silent for another moment. "OK, listeners, I'm looking down on Broad Street right now, and I have to tell you I don't see a thing. I'm leaning out the window and I've got a good clear view of City Hall to the west and the statehouse to the east, and it looks to me like the streets are pretty empty. I'm hoping that means... ah, I don't even want to say it, but right now I'm hoping this is just some kind of sick hoax, and if it is I have to say it's in remarkably poor taste. I'd hope my listeners wouldn't— *Jesus!*"

For a few seconds we hear nothing but Barry's panicked breathing.

"*Somebody jumped!*" His calm, collected radio voice has gone now. "Somebody jumped, or, or, or was pushed, or something. I just saw a person fall right past my window and down to the street. I can't see where they landed or what happened but... Oh mother of God, there's more of them! Friends, I'm looking over at the Doubletree Hotel just a block to the south of the studio and I'm seeing jumpers from the parking structure." Barry's voice seems to slur a little, like he's had a couple of drinks. "They're... oh God, they're just leaping from the garage levels, four, five floors above the street. Some of them are... Jesus, some of them are getting back up again. They're just... they're getting up from the ground and they're chasing the... oh no, something's..." He sounds completely drunk now. "I can see it on the window. Little, umm... little... I'm having a little trouble here. Can't... can't think of the, umm... the words. It's... little, umm, droplets." For a few moments all we hear is his breathing, them his voice returns a final time. Small. Quiet. Sad.

"Oh no."

He drifts off, and for the length of a dozen heartbeats there's nothing but a rustling sound. The mic against clothing? Then more heavy breathing. Deep. Irregular.

Now a noise that sounds like the inside of a wind tunnel, a rushing roar.

Now a dull thud.

Now nothing. Silence.

Samuel Whelan sits slumped over the long rosewood table in the situation room, head in hands, avoiding the sight of the big screen on the wall. Every few seconds a new red dot blooms on the map. Albuquerque. Bakersfield. Salt Lake City. Seattle. Each new dot represents a successful strike. Each dot means a puny little crop duster, a massive DC10 or a Bell 205 forest fire helicopter has successfully dropped its load on an unsuspecting city. Each dot represents chaos. Violence. Tens of thousands more dead and infected.

Each new dot brings with it a loud beep, and Whelan cringes with each one as if it brings him physical pain.

This was his plan. It was his brainchild, twisted and bastardized until it had become the exact opposite of what he'd intended. A thousand or so civilian, former military and emergency services pilots, each volunteering whatever craft they had available to save the country. He'd worked for weeks to corral them, getting the word out to fire departments, flight schools and private airfields across the nation to orchestrate what may be the single largest airstrike in the history of the planet.

The strike was supposed to save the country, and Whelan would have gone down in history as the architect of that miracle. Samuel Barnes Whelan, a man who'd spent his entire career tirelessly fighting for the interests of his nation. This would have been his crowning glory, the ultimate bloodless coup, as countless cities were bathed in a lifesaving vaccine that stopped *Cordyceps bangkokii* in its tracks and took back the nation from the infection.

And then he told Lassiter about it.

Whelan spins in his chair just quickly enough to grab the trash can before vomiting. A little splashes on his suit pants but he manages to catch most of it. He spits, wipes his mouth with the back of his sleeve and turns away from the screen once again, but not before noticing the red dot over Des Moines. His home town, gone in an instant.

Terrence fucking Lassiter.

Whelan came up through the ranks as a field agent in the Eighties. He'd spent years running dangerous missions all across the globe, and his service record was so heavily redacted it was basically just a binder of black paper with his name on the front page. He'd come face to face with everyone from Afghan Mujahideen to North Korean spies to Colombian cartel kingpins. He'd fought the worst of the worst, serious bad guys, and he'd lived to tell the tale.

In all those years as a field agent, a desk warrior and a shrewd political operator in the Washington machine he'd never come across anyone as dangerous as Terrence Lassiter. He'd heard the stories, of course. Everyone in DC had heard the stories. Lassiter was a lunatic. A fanatic. An honest to goodness religious nut, as unhinged as the worst cult leader. You couldn't trust him as far as you could throw him, and he'd happily feed you and your entire family to the lions if it helped him take a single step closer to his goals.

But everyone talked like that in DC about everyone else. Everyone threw hyperbolic insults back and forth, and everyone on the other side of the aisle was made out to be

Satan personified. That was just the reality in the capital, and the problem is that it all became a little like the way people misused the word 'literally' when they really meant 'figuratively', and they did it so much that eventually even the dictionary gave up the battle as lost.

When everyone in DC describes everyone else as Satan, how the fuck can you tell when the *real* Satan comes along? The warnings have all been devalued and watered down. They don't mean anything any more, so you just tune them out.

Lassiter is truly insane. Whelan knows that now, but it's far too late.

When he arrived from Langley on the first day everyone warned him. *Watch out for that Lassiter*, they said. *He's a power hungry son of a bitch.* Of course he ignored them. People had said the same about every President from Reagan to Howard, and most of them had turned out to be fine at the end of the day. Sure, some were a little too eager to send other people's kids to war, and others were a little too gung-ho about socialized medicine, but at the end of the day they were all just typical politicians. You wouldn't trust them to hold your wallet, but you never worried they'd line you up against the wall and give the order to fire.

It took eleven days for Whelan to finally learn the truth, and the truth came with a bullet, but once Lassiter started ordering the executions of 'traitors and defectors', as he called them, it was already far too late to get away. By that point Whelan was just riding the tiger. If he tried to leave he'd find himself before a firing squad, and that wasn't an option. Whelan was a born survivor.

No, the only viable option was to stick it out. To try to guide Lassiter as best he could in the right direction. Maybe - just maybe, and he could barely even countenance the idea - find enough allies at Site R to muster a coup. To take Lassiter out, and install a President who wasn't so obviously insane.

Operation Crop Dust was meant to be his way out. It was meant to get everyone back up to the surface where the cold light of day might allow them to regain some perspective and escape the warping influence of their plainly untethered commander in chief.

And so he'd played along with Lassiter's madness. He'd nodded and smiled like someone trying to placate an armed lunatic when Lassiter described to him his vision of a 'pure' United States. When he explained that *Cordyceps* had been a blessing in disguise. That it would allow them to clear out the deadwood, rid themselves of the cancer of liberal politics and return the nation to its rightful place as God's own country. Lassiter envisioned a vast evacuation effort in which a hand-picked group of the truly righteous were protected from the infection and safely hidden away while the rest of the country - the liberals, atheists, minorities, homosexuals and anyone else Lassiter deemed unworthy of life - tore each other apart, after which the righteous would arise from the ashes and begin to rebuild.

Obviously, it was plain to any fool that the plan was utterly abhorrent. It was pure evil but it was also completely impractical, and a great way to keep Lassiter occupied while Whelan worked around him. Lassiter could waste his time orchestrating his insane little scheme to turn the United States into his delusional wet dream, and it would buy Whelan time to find a real, plausible solution that would save the country.

He'd spent the first week as Lassiter's right hand man liaising with the doctors and scientists working at Camp One. Unlike many he actually *did* agree that it might be worth sacrificing a few thousand innocents if it meant saving the nation. He didn't like the idea - far from it - but he was a realist. He lived in a world of hard choices, and he knew from long experience that sometimes there simply weren't any good solutions. Sometimes you just had to settle for the one that promised the least degree of harm.

Site R's point man at the camp was a man named Major Ronald Armitage. He was an accomplished scientist, the Deputy Director of DARPA, the Defense Advanced Research Projects Agency, and he assured Whelan that his team would be able to find a solution. They were pursuing an extremely promising path with a newly developed clinical vaccine against *Candida*, a fungus that causes often fatal invasive infections in immuno-suppressed patients. The vaccine ruptures and breaks down the cell walls of *Candida* spores, preventing them from latching onto blood cells and blocking them from accessing the energy they need to reproduce. Before the attacks the vaccine had already been through two years of successful human trials, and it was just waiting on FDA approval.

Armitage had said there was an excellent chance the *Candida* vaccine could be fairly easily re-engineered to target *Cordyceps bangkokii.* Both fungi were extremely similar in structure and behavior, and with a little fine tuning the vaccine could be just as effective against the new threat. What's more, Armitage already knew that the *Candida* vaccine could be effectively aerosolized and was hardy enough to survive long spells outside the body, which meant it should be possible to deliver it directly to large populations by air drop. It was a beautifully elegant solution. The only things that stood in the way of immunizing the entire population against *Cordyceps* were funding, resources and time, and Whelan was more than happy to grant all three.

He failed to understand two important things. The first was that Lassiter, while delusional, wasn't nearly as oblivious to reality as Whelan assumed. The second was that Lassiter was also in direct contact with Major Armitage, and he was issuing him very different orders.

While Armitage worked to develop his vaccine, on Lassiter's orders he'd also set aside a large number of refugees to use as... the best term may be *Cordyceps* factories. Hundreds were immobilized, deliberately infected with the fungus and harvested as it multiplied within their bodies, before being dispatched and discarded in mass graves when the fungus had burned through all available energy. The stockpiles of Cordyceps were then unwittingly transported around the nation by private security forces, FEMA and what little remained of the armed forces.

When Whelan relayed the go order for Operation Crop Dust he'd been under the impression that they were delivering the vaccine. Armitage had assured him it was ready, and was being stockpiled and distributed. He'd lied to him, on Lassiter's orders.

Samuel Barnes Whelan had, about two hours earlier, unwittingly ordered the wholesale slaughter of millions of his fellow Americans. He'd sentenced millions to death with a single phone call, and thanks to Lassiter's lies he'd snatched defeat from the jaws of victory.

That's why, on the lustrous rosewood table in front of him, just beside the phone he used to relay the order, sits a small folding knife, and beside it two clear glass vials. They're just tiny things, not much larger than a sample sized bottle of cologne. There aren't even any markings on them. There's nothing at all to suggest what's inside.

He steels himself for a moment before turning to the wall screen, takes a look at the countless dots still spreading across the United States, and says a silent prayer for the many millions of people he unwittingly condemned. He knows he'll never be able to truly atone for his sins, but while those he killed will never know it he'd like to think they'd approve of what comes next.

Whelan takes a sip of water, pushes back his chair, slips the knife in his pocket and closes his fist carefully over one of the vials. He straightens his tie, steps to the air conditioning duct at the wall, opens the cap and pours the other through the grating. He knows the system will carry the contents efficiently around the complex within an hour or so.

The other vial is just for him.

He walks to the door and nods politely to the guard on the way out. At this time of night the hallways are virtually empty, the lights dimmed to simulate the same kind of day/night cycle as up on the surface, but he can see from the glow at the foot of the door that the chapel lights are burning bright. Lassiter's in there, praying to a God he truly believes with all his heart would condone his actions.

Whelan pushes open the door and steps through into the light. It's only his second time in the chapel. He's not a particularly religious man. It's difficult to keep the faith in his line of work, and what tattered scraps of belief remained after all these years were decisively burned away over the last month.

He doesn't fear eternal judgment. He just wants an end to the suffering.

Lassiter rests on his knees by the front row of pews, silently praying and oblivious to Whelan's presence. He doesn't hear Whelan approach until it's far too late.

Samuel Barnes Whelan was trained in close combat as a CIA field agent. It may have been twenty years since he last needed to draw on that training, but it's like riding a bicycle. You never really forget. Lassiter turns at the sound of Whelan's loafers squeaking on the tile floor. His eyes widen in fear as he sees the hate radiating from his right hand man, but before he can open his mouth to cry out Whelan thrusts the heel of his palm into Lassiter's throat.

The old man falls back and wheezes, struggling to breathe. It will be difficult, but he'll be able to take in enough air to stay alive. That's important to Whelan. He wants Lassiter awake and aware. He just doesn't want him to be able to call for a guard.

Lassiter tries to scramble to his feet, clutching the marble pulpit with his bony fingers. Whelan slips the folding knife from his pocket, leans down, takes hold of Lassiter's right calf and calmly slices his Achilles' tendon. The President lets out a wheezing breath, trying to scream but unable to get it out. Whelan ignores him, grips his left leg and repeats the process.

"Don't try to talk," he says, his voice low and calm. "It's time to listen, Terrence." He looks down into Lassiter's wide, terrified, bloodshot eyes, staring at his own useless feet as blood seeps from the wounds. "Don't worry, you won't bleed to death. I know what I'm doing."

Whelan lowers himself into a pew and crosses one leg over the other. "Now, do you know what's going to happen next? No? Well, Terrence, you're going to die." He rests his hand on his thigh, palm facing up, takes the bloodied knife and runs a long line across his hand, wincing with the pain. Lassiter stares at the cut with tears in his eyes, his mouth opening and closing silently.

"You know you'll be the first man I ever killed, Terrence. Directly, at least. You know, face to face. All those years as an agent and I never had to take a life. Never had to slip poison into a drink. Never had to take out a double agent. I know, right? I wasn't exactly James Bond." He opens his fist and shows Lassiter the glass vial. "Tonight you made me kill millions, and none of them will be clean deaths."

He tosses the vial into his cut hand and crushes it in his fist. A little blood runs down his wrist and stains his white shirt sleeve red. "Millions of terrified people, Terrence. Chased. Beaten to death. Torn to shreds by their own loved ones. So," he says, relaxing in the pew," I think it's only fair that their commander in chief joins them."

Whelan blinks a couple of times and shakes his head. He can already feel the effects of the *Cordyceps* coursing through his veins. He feels lightheaded and a little sleepy, just as he does whenever he sits in a meeting after a scotch at lunch. "It's kicking in, Terrence. Not long to wait now. It'll all be over soon."

Lassiter reaches up to the pulpit and grabs at the corner of a copy of the Bible until it falls down to his chest. He hugs it close, as if it might offer some kind of protection. Whelan chuckles. "You really thought you were serving God, Terrence? You really thought God wanted you to kill millions of His people? No, Terrence, you weren't serving God. You were only serving yourself. God would be disgusted with you. He'd be ashamed to have let a self-righteous maggot like you soil his creation." He feels a tingling in his limbs, and a touch of vertigo kicks in. "He's going to let you die down here in the darkness, Terrence. You'll never feel the sun on your face again. That's your reward, Terrence. That's your punishment... Oh... I feel it. It's time, Terrence. I hope you're ready to face whatever comes next."

Beside the door of the situation room the young guard stands to attention, struggling to stay awake in the half light. For the last half hour he's been counting the floor tiles, trying to stay alert by working out the volume of water it would take to flood the hallway up to the ceiling, assuming the floor tiles are six inches to a side. So far he's—

He has his gun out of its holster moments after hearing the scream. It sounds like a wounded animal, more a roar than a scream.

He rushes in the direction of the chapel, bursting through the door just in time to see Samuel Whelan lower his head to the body in front of the pulpit. He freezes in terror as Whelan takes a bite, and comes back up with a length of stringy, bloody flesh stretching from his teeth down to the body.

The guard puts him down in two shots, the first through his back and the second a clean shot through the back of the head. Whelan slumps to the ground like a rag doll, and the guard rushes forward and turns white as a sheet as he sees the President beneath him.

He mumbles a few words into his radio, and moments later a siren begins to wail through the facility, echoing through the halls, locking down each section of the site and allowing only guards free movement. He'll just wait at the door and keep the room secure until backup arrives. He'll—

Beneath Whelan's body the President begins to stir. It's just a twitch at first, but then he struggles to pull himself up. The guard rushes back towards the pulpit, desperately struggling to remember the first aid training he was given during basic. How do you treat a neck wound? Apply pressure, right? Raise the head above the body?

He's only a few feet from the President when he realizes first aid won't do any good.

President Terrence Lassiter opens and closes his mouth, letting out a strained snarl from his collapsed throat. He locks his bloodshot eyes on the guard and reaches his hands out towards him, desperately trying to attack but held back by the weight of Whelan's body covering his legs.

The guard raises his gun without a second thought and calmly puts a bullet through the President's left eye. The man slumps to the ground, and as he falls the Bible slips from his chest and lands with a splash in the spreading pool of blood surrounding his head like a halo.

Warren hunts through the AM band with a somber expression, visibly tensing whenever he finds something other than static. He's wearing earphones to pick up the weaker, more distant signals, and reporting to us whenever he finds something. In the last hour he's tuned into more than a dozen broadcasters from all across the country - KAAY out of Little Rock; KVOX, Fargo; WMVP, Chicago, to name a few - and they're each reporting the same thing. There's been a widespread outbreak in every state we've heard from, and while we can scarcely believe it it seems to have been intentional. Five of the stations reported sightings of aircraft above towns and cities before everything went to shit.

Bishop has been weeping in the corner for the last twenty minutes, and I don't blame him at all. A little while ago Warren picked up a faint signal from WJOX, a 50kW sports radio station out of Birmingham, Alabama, his home town. The DJ reported in a thick, slow southern drawl that a DC10 had dropped what looked like water across a huge swathe of the city, including the broadcast studio itself. We held the signal for ten minutes, and by the time it finally cut out the DJ was begging for help as the infected swarmed in from the street through the broken window.

Bishop's family is long gone, thank God, but I still understand how he feels. I felt the exact same way when I stood on the Verrazano Narrows bridge and looked back at the ruins of Brooklyn. It's not so much the destruction. That's just the most obvious aspect of the tragedy.

No, the biggest tragedy is learning that everything you ever knew is forever gone. It's the thought that no matter how long you live you really can't ever go home again. The city might still remain. Bishop's old high school might still stand, and his childhood home might look just the same as it always did. The same rusty gate out front. The same creaking floorboard on the third step up the staircase. The same old tire swing in the back yard. But none of it matters without the people. Without the people they're just buildings.

So now, like me, he's set adrift. Even if we can somehow survive this, whatever it is. Even if we can get through it unharmed until the very last of the infected die away, where is there to go? To where would we return after our victory? Soldiers at least get to go home after surviving a brutal war, but for us there's nowhere to return to. We've not only lost our future, but our connection to the past.

"Tom?" Warren tugs at my sleeve. "Help me out here, man, this signal's real weak. Here, take an ear." He hands over one of his earbuds, and carefully plays with the dial to try to hunt down the signal. I can hear a voice, just barely. "You hearing that?"

I nod, and press the earbud deeper into my ear in an effort to pick it up more clearly.

"— the order from up top a couple hours ago, but something didn't seem right so we held off."

"That's it, Warren. I got it, don't touch the dial."

Another voice comes through. Sounds like she's from somewhere out west. "Captain, when you say you got orders, where exactly did they come from? Is there still a command structure in place?"

"Well not really, ma'am, at least not as far as I know. The way I understand it the orders come direct from the President. Or, you know, someone at the base near Camp David, anyhow. All I know is that we've been speaking to a man by the name of Whelan these past two weeks. I'm told he's the boss at the CIA, and he had all the right authorization codes to order an airdrop, so we went along with it."

The woman returns. "And can you tell us exactly what happened tonight, in your own words?"

"Yes, ma'am. I came on shift 'bout two hours ago to find we'd received a shipment of vaccine from... well, I don't know, to tell the truth, but it was delivered in a kinda gas truck by folks who identified themselves as army, and they had all the right ID, so we let 'em fill three of our Bambi buckets. They handed me orders to make the drop at midnight local time, and—"

"I'm sorry, Captain, Bambi buckets?"

"That's right, ma'am. That's what we call the, ah, the water containers we use to make drops over wildfires. They're just collapsible open topped buckets. We usually dip them down into Kirby Lake to fill 'em up, dump them on a fire then head back to fill 'em up again." He coughs. "So anyway, they gave me orders to make all three drops at the same time over Abilene, which is... well, I don't know, something about it didn't scan quite right, then I noticed the guys pumping the vaccine were wearing respirators. Just didn't seem above board, you know?"

"And Captain," the woman asks, "did you question the orders at the time?"

"No, ma'am, I didn't. There was just something off about them, you know, and the way things have been recently I didn't want to find myself in a fight with a bunch of tooled up creeps, you know? So yeah, I just took the orders and sent them on their way, then I tried to put in a call in to Whelan over there at Site R, but I couldn't get through to the switchboard until gone half past midnight, when they told me that all orders were rescinded until further notice. They wouldn't tell me what the hell was goin' on, but they just warned me to stay the hell away from those Bambi buckets. Of course, then we started to hear about what was going on elsewhere. All I can say is thank Christ we held off. I just don't think I could have lived with myself if I'd dropped that stuff on my family. Doesn't bear thinking about, does it?"

"It doesn't, Captain. I want to thank you for taking the time to speak with us tonight, and I'm sure everyone in Abilene thanks you for your caution. God bless, Captain."

"Well, thank you, ma'am, I appreciate it."

"That was Captain Roy Walken of the Abilene Fire Department, whose brave actions tonight surely saved the lives of more than a hundred thousand residents of Abilene, Texas." She pauses for a moment, as if to collect her thoughts, and lets out a heavy sigh. "Folks, it's been a rough night here in the Lone Star State, and all across the country. We don't know much, and details are still emerging by the minute, but we know that the nation has been dealt an almost killing blow with widespread attacks on dozens of cities and hundreds of towns from coast to coast. We're also hearing rumors - and I'd like to make it clear that they are, at present, unconfirmed - that an attempted coup at the government facility Site R has resulted in the death of Acting President Lassiter. We're doing everything we can to firm up that information for you right now, but right now we can't seem to raise contact with the facility. As it stands we're..." The voice suddenly fades out.

"What did you do? Get it back!" I demand.

Warren shrugs. "I didn't do anything, the battery died." He sighs. "I got some more in the car, but unless somebody wants to ring the dinner bell for the dozen or so hungry fuckers down on the street it'll have to wait until morning."

Over in the corner Vee's trying to coax Bishop out of his depression with a candy bar, and strangely enough it seems to be doing the trick. He's stopped crying, at least. "Hey, guys?" I call out quietly. Vee looks up while Bishop struggles with the wrapper of a Three Musketeers bar. "Word is the President's dead."

I don't know what I expected. Joy? Relief? I've no idea, but I didn't expect anger. Vee looks furious, as if she's personally offended that she won't get the chance to kill him herself. She makes a fist and punches the wall beside Bishop, making the big guy flinch away from her and drop his candy bar. "Fucking piece of shit coward prick, dying in his bunker like a God damned cut price Hitler. I wanted to string him up above a pit full of infected, hand a knife to the families of everyone who died in that camp and watch him beg for fucking mercy. *Jesus*," she sighs and slumps against the wall beside Bishop.

Warren and I exchange a look. "Warren, let's never get on her bad side, OK?"

He chuckles. "Hey, you don't have to tell me, brother. Couple weeks ago she pushed a guy off the roof of a 7-Eleven for bleeding on her boots."

"Infected, right?"

He shrugs and gives me a sly smile. "Well, she said he was, but..."

"He was infected," Vee testily insists. "I just really loved those boots, OK? Had to throw the damned things out once they got covered in infected blood." She looks down at her heavy standard issue boots and breaks the slightest hint of a smile. "This apocalypse has been murder on my wardrobe."

Warren smiles and tucks the dead radio back in his duffel. "Well kids, I'd love to stay up all night and regale you with gory stories about the trail of dead Lieutenant Reyes has left in her wake, but I think it's a good idea for us all to get a little shut eye. Come morning we have to make some big decisions, and I don't want you guys all cranky and uptight while we're planning how to stay alive." He lifts himself from the floor and hikes his rifle up over his shoulder. "I'll take first watch."

I glance at my wrist, as if the time of night really matters any more. "I think I'll join you for a while if you don't mind. Don't think I'll be able to get much sleep, knowing what's outside."

Warren nods. "Yeah, it takes a little getting used to, I'll grant you that. Come on, I think I've got a little scotch in my pack. That should help knock you out."

"You good, Vee?" I look over to Reyes to find her smiling, leaning against Bishop's large, pillow-like shoulders. "Yeah, go ahead. This might be the best night's sleep I'll get in weeks. Bishop here's like a big teddy bear."

Bishop flashes a cheerful grin, his mouth surrounded with a ring of melted chocolate, and shuffles his ass forward until he's resting comfortably against the wall. "Huh huh," he chuckles, closing his eyes. "Teddy bear."

"Good night, guys." I grab my jacket, turn the knob on the lamp until the light fades, and follow Warren down the corridor back to the front of the building, glad for the opportunity to take a little fresh air.

"After a month locked in that box this is something I'll never take for granted again," I say, heading straight for the window.

"What's that?"

"Air. Just... fresh damned air, whenever I feel like taking a breath. You don't miss the breeze on your face until it's gone, you know? All I want to do now is go live in the middle of a big, open field and just live under the stars, feeling the breeze."

Warren smiles. "Me, I just wanna get a nice little yacht and find some island somewhere. I don't care where, as long as it doesn't stink of dead people." He tugs a bottle from the depths of his duffel and tosses it over. Lagavulin, 16 years old. "Thanks." I nod appreciatively. "Hey, this is good stuff."

"Yeah? I boosted it from a liquor store out in Valley Lake. I'm not a big liquor drinker, to be honest. I just grabbed the bottle with the biggest price tag."

"Good call." I unscrew the cap and take a long swig, enjoying the warmth as it coats the sides of my throat like honey. "This is my drink, when I can afford to switch from beer." I hand it back, and try to resist the urge to laugh at Warren's expression as he takes a gulp of the burning liquor.

"Jesus," he groans, wiping his mouth. "People drink this shit for fun? Gimme a cold beer any day of the week."

I take the bottle back from him. "It's an acquired taste, but if you ever want to get drunk again I'd advise you to acquire it. I get the feeling the future isn't so bright for cold beer." I take another swig and lower myself down against the wall by the window. I'm already feeling the whiskey kick in after a month without touching a drop. "So what's your story, Warren? How'd you end up on the wrong end of the apocalypse?"

He grabs an office chair in the darkness, rolling it over by the window so he can see out to the street. "My story? Well, it doesn't take much telling. Typical army brat. I spent a lot of time following my dad around the world as a kid. Little time in Germany. Couple of years at Okinawa. *Far* too much time in Guam. Soldiering is the family business, so when the time came I joined up.

Trained as a sniper at Fort Benning, then it was straight off to Afghanistan, then Syria. Three tours, 107 confirmed kills." He reaches over and takes back the bottle. "I never really cared for it, to be honest. I always wanted to be a firefighter, but what are you gonna do? Turns out I'm just really good at killing people from far away." He winces again at the burn, then sighs. "Anyway, I took an IED hit near Damascus just back in March. They shipped me off back home, and I'd just about had the last piece of shrapnel pulled out of my ass in Maryland when everything started to go south. I checked myself out, found a ride north, hooked up with Vee's unit from Fort Dix and the rest is history. We spent the last month on cleanup duty, trying and failing to get some kind of handle on this mess."

Another pull, another wince. "Gah! That shit's awful." He hands it back again. "We bugged out after Vee's husband was killed last week, when we found out what was really going on at Camp One. Figured it was best to carry on solo after we realized who we were really fighting for." He falls silent and takes a long look out the window, scanning the street below. "What about you? What did you do before all this shit?"

I pull out my cigarettes. "Do you mind if I...?" Warren shakes his head, and I light up. "Well, before all this I guess I was a professional drifter, if we're being honest." I take another swig, and I'm surprised to realize I'm already getting pretty drunk. "I was a freelance journalist. I traveled around the world picking up work here and there. Mostly small stuff, you know, local papers, airline magazines, that kinda thing. I wasn't great, but I made enough cash that I could live pretty well in Asia and avoid growing up for as long as possible.

"I was in Thailand last year, just a couple of months after the first attack. You remember that guy Paul McQueen? The Aussie guy who survived it? I knew him. Just by chance he and I used to be drinking buddies in Ulaanbaatar, Mongolia, and when he decided to tell his story he reached out to me. I guess I might have talked up my career a little after a few beers one time, and he thought I was some kind of serious newsman. You know, rather than a guy who wrote articles like *15 Budget Breaks in*

Sweden for Scandinavian Airlines' in-flight magazine.

"That got me a feature in Time Magazine. My first big story, and it ended with an old friend killing himself." I take a long drag on the Marlboro, and watch the smoke curl away in the dim moonlight. "After that I guess I went a little off the rails for a while. Came home to New York and spent months obsessing about that warning. You remember it, that weird handwritten message from the Sons of the Father? That thing scared me. I got caught up in all kinds of conspiracy theories, trying to prove it was genuine, but I didn't know how. I guess I went a little too far down the rabbit hole. Started to lose track of what was real." I can tell I'm slurring my words a little now.

"Then one day I met a girl. Kate. Just a regular girl, nothing all that special about her. I wasn't in love with her. Didn't really have all that much in common with her, to be honest, but she was *safe*. I figured if I just acted liked I was in love I might magically end up leading some kind of normal life. You know, move in with her. Get a rescue dog. Argue about which IKEA bookcase best suits our personalities. I managed to fool myself for months." I take another long swig and pass the already half empty bottle up to Warren.

"Don't let me have any more of that." I stub out my cigarette on the carpet and continue. "When New York went to shit we got caught up right in the middle of it. We ended up at a park in Brooklyn, just... just *rammed* with people. Thousands of them, all terrified and confused. When we heard there were bombs on the way we tried to get out, and... well, the details aren't important, but it all went wrong. Kate died."

I look up at the weaving image of Warren at the window and take a deep breath. "You know the first thought that went through my head when I realized she'd been killed? I was *relieved*. I was fucking relieved that I didn't have to play at being a regular person any more. *Jesus* fucking Christ, I'm going to hell."

Warren takes a sip from the bottle and remains diplomatically silent.

"That's what's been rattling around my head for the last month. Stuck in that box, wondering why an asshole like me deserved to live while a sweet girl like Kate deserved to die. Where's the justice in that? She was too good for me. She loved me, and I couldn't even keep her safe." I reach for my pack of smokes, then remember I just put one out. "Anyway... I don't know why I'm here. I don't know why I survived and she didn't, and I don't have the first fucking clue how I can ever redeem myself."

My mind finally clears long enough for me to realize I'm heaping my innermost worries on someone I've only known for a few hours. I look around in the darkness for my jacket and pull over my legs. "Umm... I think I need to rest my eyes a little."

"Yeah, I think that's probably a good idea, Tom. Don't worry, I'll hold the fort. You just get some sleep. You'll feel much better in the morning."

"Yeah. Yeah, it'll all be better in the morning. Thanks, Warren. You're a good guy." I roll to the side, tuck my legs up towards my chest and pull the jacket a little further up. "Better in the morning," I mutter to myself.

The darkness only takes a few moments to close in.

It had been three days since a car last went by, and he was growing impatient. He was hungry. He was tired. He hadn't been laid in more than a week. If he didn't find someone soon he'd die before they let him back in. Jesus, he might never get laid again.

The community was pretty simple. You get to sleep somewhere safe and warm, and maybe you get the chance to take a turn with one of the women every once in a while, but only if you deliver the goods. Bring in loot to share and you get to stay. Come home empty handed and you're on your own. Sounds like a perfect system. Fair work for fair pay. No damned welfare queens suckling at the teat of hard working folk like Roy. No scroungers taking what was rightfully his. No assholes to abuse the generosity of good, honest, decent people.

It was just what he'd been hoping for all these years. It was what he'd prayed for whenever someone shared yet another story on Facebook about some entitled asshole buying lobster with his food stamps, or a damned immigrant family being handed a free home bigger than his just because the mom couldn't stop firing out kids. Roy had been over the moon when he finally got his wish. Work hard and you're on easy street. Slack off and you're out on your ass. No free rides. That's the way it should be. We can't afford to support folk who don't pull their weight. You don't want to work? Tough shit.

The community had been pretty great in the beginning, back when the quarantine zone was first established. The place was set up pretty quickly after people started evacuating, and with only thirty or so residents its needs were simple. Guns, food, and clean water. Maybe a little medicine, just in case. With millions of fugees fleeing to the west and no cops on the streets the pickings were easy. Roy worked just a couple hours a day. He'd get up, head out, raid an abandoned Walmart, and he'd be back home before lunch with a trunk full of canned soup and a few crates of vodka.

Then it all began to change. The community grew, and it started taking in people who had real skills. The doc arrived, and he was exempt from looting. A couple of plumbers came in, and they got the same treatment 'cause they knew how to keep the showers working with some fancy pumps. An electrician showed up - a damned wetback, at that - and he was given a pass 'cause he knew how to set up solar power up on the roof so they didn't have to run the generators day and night. And the women, of course. They were let in for free so long as they were willing to give it up every so often.

It was only a few weeks before there were ten times as many mouths to feed. More than four hundred people behind the walls, and suddenly they decided old Roy wasn't doing his part. "You only got a hundred tins today, Roy?" they'd say, looking down their noses like the fancy assholes sitting at the top of the pile always did to good, honest people like him. "We got hundreds of mouths to feed in here, man. We need at least a thousand tins every day just to keep folks fed. You're gonna have to go out again."

He tried to keep it up for a while. Worked four, five hours a day collecting loot. Tried to find new stores that hadn't already been picked clean. Tried to lug enough crap home that he'd get a pat on the head and the satisfaction of a job well done, but it was never enough for those bastards. They always wanted more. They always wanted to exploit his hard work just a little too much.

So... yeah. Suddenly good old Roy found himself surplus to requirements, just like he had in every damned job for the last ten years. There were fifty folk out looting for the community, and they said he was the laziest. They said he drank more'n he brought back, and he was taking more'n his share of food and smokes. They said he took too much time with the women, and if he wanted more he'd have to work harder to earn it.

Of course it was bullshit. Roy pulled his weight just like everyone else. He broke his back to provide for his new family, but like always folks like Roy just weren't appreciated. There was always some asshole up at the top who'd try to take advantage of simple hard working folk like him.

The last straw came one day when he'd just finished up with one of the girls, sometime around lunchtime. He was just about to wash up and go on a looting run when the top guy

- some jumped up prick who called himself the Chief - stormed in and grabbed hold of his collar. He dragged Roy down to the front door, threw his bag out into the street and tossed Roy after it. Kept going on about how they needed the beds for people who worked hard for them. Wouldn't even listen when Roy said he was just heading out the door to go to work.

He still wanted back in, though. Even after just a week he was already tired of sleeping with one eye open. He was tired of washing with cold bottled water. He was tired of having to find somewhere to rest each night where he knew they couldn't get at him. Everything was better at the community, even if it was run by silver spoon pricks who wouldn't know a day of hard work if it married their sister.

Then he figured out what he could bring to the table. He figured out how he could get back through the door.

There were a little more than four hundred people in the community when he left, but only around forty women. When everyone ran away to the west it was mostly the guys who stayed behind. People with families were long gone. You're not gonna keep your wife and kids in Pennsylvania when there are crazy infected fuckers running around the place, so of course they were the first to go, tearing away in their sensible SUVs with SpongeBob playing on the screens in the back of the seats.

The guys who stuck around were mostly young, ambitious types. Guys with vision and balls. Guys who could see the opportunities presented by the quarantine zone. They were mostly single, and of course they all liked to get laid.

Now, some of those forty women in the community were a little too old, or a lot too young. The law didn't hold much weight any more but the Chief had made it pretty damned clear from day one that nobody was to touch the kids and grandmas. That only left one woman for every twenty or so men, and by the time they kicked Roy out the girls were already whining about being worked too hard for their keep.

So... yeah. There was Roy's way back in. They'd have to open the doors for him if he brought back a fresh, tasty piece of pussy to share around. They'd slap him on the back and call him a hero. Maybe he'd earn himself a couple weeks grace. A couple weeks to sit back and relax in safety before they started asking more from him. A couple weeks to try out the rest of the girls. Hell, maybe they'd be so grateful he took some work off their plate they'd throw him a little extra.

But there was a problem. He didn't know where to find any fucking women.

He'd been out on the road for a week, and he'd yet to see a single chick. He'd looked high and low, scouring houses out in the sticks, visiting all the old FEMA camps to see if there were any stragglers left behind. He found plenty of guys and plenty more infected, but no pussy.

Then he had a brainwave. The highway.

The 78 was pretty much the only east-west highway still clear. Most of the other routes got snarled up with breakdowns and pile ups the first few days when all the fugees fled west, but the 78 wasn't so bad. It came from the direction of New York, and... well, most of the folks from New York were already dead.

So Roy decided to camp out. He stocked up on food and water, found himself a pair of binoculars and set himself up on a hill close to a curve in the highway where cars would have to slow down to pass a pile of wrecks. He figured eventually he'd get lucky. Eventually a couple of stragglers would decide the east was too risky, and they'd try to make it out west by the highway. There had to be a few women left, and when they came by he'd pounce. It was a solid plan, and he was pretty damned proud of himself for dreaming it up.

Then three days went by.

Three days without a single car. Three days staring down at an empty road, sleeping up a tree with a branch sticking into his spine just in case any infected came by at night. Three days without a wash, and a day since his cigarettes had run out. He was about ready to call it quits, drive back to the community and just beg them to open the doors. He'd clean toilets. He'd scrub dishes. He'd go out looting ten, twelve hours a day. He'd do just about anything if it meant he could sleep in safety again.

He'd decided to make a move as soon as the sun came up after his fourth night in the tree. He'd stop in at a Target he'd seen close to the highway and return with a car stocked to the roof with goodies. Candy, cigarettes, booze and enough tinned food to feed an army. He'd camp outside for a week if necessary, pleading with them to open the doors. It was all set.

It was sometime around one in the morning when he heard the engine. For a moment he thought he was imagining it. The only sounds he'd heard in days were the wind, the groans of the infected and the report from his own pistol as he burned through his dwindling supply of ammo. He rolled down the window, cocked his ear and held his breath as he listened for it.

There it was, right on the edge of his hearing, drifting in and out as the wind carried it. He scrambled quickly from his car and climbed to the roof, grabbing his binoculars as he went. It took him a moment to find it but there it was, an old, beat up Toyota puttering slowly through the wrecks.

And there was a woman driving.

He could barely believe his luck. He hadn't seen a woman out in the wild for about three weeks, and to be honest it was really weird to see one just sitting in a car, driving around like she wasn't an endangered species.

Not only was it a woman but she looked pretty hot, far as he could tell. Slim, nice lips, decent set of tits. It wasn't so easy to see in the darkness but she looked like she might be a Spic. Roy didn't really go for Mexican chicks, but he knew a lot of people went crazy for the exotic types. She'd go down a storm back at the community. They didn't get all that many of them in rural Pennsylvania, and most of the women back at the community were white as snow apart from one light-skinned black chick with a smart mouth and a fat ass. The folks back home'd just eat up that sweet Latina pussy, so long as she was one of the clean ones.

He scanned the rest of the car through his binoculars, and he was a little put off by the fact that there were a few guys in the car. The big guy in the back looked like he could be trouble. No telling with the other two. They both looked smaller than Roy, but who knows? Sometimes those wiry guys could throw a solid punch. Might be a good idea to take all three of them out if the chance came up.

He jumped back in the car and gunned the engine, fishtailing it with the lights off until he finally skidded his way down onto a dusty track that ran alongside the highway a while. He tried to keep his speed under control. He was getting a little too excited, and he knew the Toyota would easily outpace him once it worked its way through the wrecks. If he could just get to the next on ramp before it vanished he might be able to trail them until they took a break.

His heart leaped to his throat when he saw the car peel off the highway at the next exit. It was coming right towards him, so he cut off the engine and sat in wait while it rolled slowly into the next town. He followed carefully, making sure he didn't get too close, until they parked up in front of an old office block and started unpacking their car.

Mm hmm, she was hot. He got a much better view once she stepped out of the car, and he definitely wasn't disappointed. She was one of those cute, spunky Michelle Rodriguez types. All tough on the surface with her heavy, shapeless army gear, but he could tell she'd be sweet and warm as apple pie underneath. There was definitely a cute little ass hiding beneath those fatigues, and even though he wasn't a big fan of the wetbacks he'd love to hold her down and spend a little time getting to know her. Hell, it was a long drive back to the community. Maybe he'd be able to find somewhere safe and quiet along the way to break her in for a while before he shared her with the rest of the guys.

He gave it a couple hours before making his move. He was eager to go earlier, but the sound of the Toyota had attracted a few infected to the street and he had to wait for them to wander away. Couldn't fire off the weapon without letting the girl know he was coming, so he had to be patient.

Finally the last of them drifted off down the street, and Roy made his move. He left the car where it was parked - it was a busted up old wreck anyhow - and skirted the buildings until he reached the car, grinning when he saw they'd left the keys in the ignition. Perfect.

Roy pulled out his pistol and checked the magazine. Only two shots left. Not enough to take out all three of the guys, but if could be enough to get the upper hand if it came to it. He slipped quietly through the open front door of the building, careful to stick to the silence of the carpet, and slowly began to make his way up the stairs.

Boy, they'd be proud of him when he got this sweet little piece of ass back to the community.

I open my eyes slowly, and immediately look around in the darkness for the cat that took a shit in my mouth.

The headache hits me right away. After a month without a drink and nothing lining my stomach but a candy bar the liquor coursed through my blood like poison, and now it's mounting a full frontal assault directly behind my left eye. It feels like my brain swelled two sizes in my sleep, and it's trying to escape through the socket.

By the window Warren lies asleep, resting against the sill, his arm draped over the stock of his rifle. On the floor beside him the bottle of Lagavulin has fallen on its side, and Warren's olive green duffel now rests in the middle of a patch of sticky carpet. I kick my jacket from my body, climb shakily to my feet and grab the bag, searching through it until I find a bottle of water and a blister pack of paracetamol. Thank God for the well-prepared.

My bladder starts calling out to me as soon as I finish the water, and in the dim blue predawn glow I clumsily make my way out of the room to the bathroom at the far end of the hallway. It's pitch black inside, so I grab a trash can and prop open the door before stumbling to the urinal, fumbling with my pants and releasing a pungent, worryingly dark stream of piss. I make a mental note to drink as much water as I can find today. They only gave us a small glass with each meal at the camp, so Bishop and I are probably both pretty severely dehydrated.

I'm shaking off when I hear the moan, and I freeze instantly. The hairs on the back of my neck stand on end, and I realize how stupid it was to leave the Beretta in my jacket pocket by the window. I'm standing in a room with only one exit, cock out, unarmed and hungover. The moan comes again, closer this time, along with the sound of wet, rasping breath. I zip up and scan the room for a weapon, but the only thing that isn't screwed down is the flimsy plastic trash can. I tiptoe to the door and grab it anyway. Maybe I can wedge it over the head of anyone who enters, blinding them long enough to get past and run back to my gun.

The moan is just outside the door now, a few steps down the hall. I flip the trash can, and I'm ready to pounce when the moan turns to soft weeping. *What the fuck?* I risk a quick peek around the door.

"Bishop, what the hell happened?" The big guy is leaning with one hand against the wall, clutching his nose and crying with pain. Tears stream down his face, and his swollen nose is a mess of blood and bubbling mucus. "Jesus, come here. Let's get you cleaned up."

Bishop nods and lets me guide him to the washbasin. I turn the faucet and wait, and it takes a moment of creaking and bubbling from the pipes before I remember the water isn't running any more. All that escapes from the faucet is a thin trickle of brackish brown liquid, so I pull Bishop over to a stall and sit him down while I lift the lid from the cistern.

He winces and moans as I wash the blood from his face, trying to squirm out of the way as I splash him. "Hold still, Bishop," I order, but still he twists away from me like a kid.

"It hurts too bad," he cries, digging his chin into his armpit so I can't reach his nose.

"OK, no more water. Lemme just get a look at your nose, man." He shakes his head and tucks it deeper. "Just lemme look at it, and I'll get you some painkillers."

After a moment's thought he finally untucks his chin and turns towards me, looking down with crossed eyes at his bloody nose. "It's real bad, Tom. I think it's broken."

"Yeah, no shit." There's a large bulge sticking out of the right side, and the tip is curved about a quarter inch to the left. I can tell by his voice and the blood and mucus bubbling from one nostril that the other is completely blocked. I know what I have to do. I've reset my own nose twice before, and I know he'll thank me in about ten minutes when the pain begins to fade.

Before Bishop figures out what I'm doing I reach out, press both thumbs firmly into the sides of his nose and pull down. With a dull, wet click the bones and cartilage shift straight, and Bishop jerks back against the cistern with a snorting cough that sends a massive amount of blood spraying across both of us.

"*Fuck!*" he yells, blowing a strand of phlegmy blood onto his shirt. "What the hell did you do that for?"

I reach behind him and rinse my hands in the cistern, then rush to the towel dispenser and grab enough paper to wipe myself down. "I fixed it," I gasp, trying to hold back the puke climbing my throat at the sight of the wet, gooey red phlegm dripping from my shirt. I grab another wad of towels and pass them to him. "Now stop whining and tell me what happened."

Bishop wipes his face and sniffs away the tears. "I thought it was a bad dream, Tom. I just thought I was imagining it, then I woke up with this," he says, pointing at his swollen face.

"What do you mean? How did it happen?"

He sniffs again. "A man came in, sometime in the night. I just woke up and he was right there in front of me with his gun. I thought he was gonna shoot me but he just turned it around and hit me in the nose and I fell down. Then he hit me on top of my head." He tilts his head towards me and gingerly pushes aside his hair. There's an angry purple lump just above his hairline. "I must have passed out, because next thing I knew it was starting to get light out in the hallway and Vee was gone."

It takes a few moments for this to sink in. "Vee's gone?"

Bishop nods mournfully. "Uh huh. Her bag's still here, but she took her gun with her."

I lean down and grab him by the shoulders. "Bishop, the man. Did he take Vee?"

He shrugs, and the tears begin again as he rubs the lump on his head. "I don't know, Tom. He knocked me out, you know?"

"OK, just... just don't do anything. I'm going to get Warren."

My hangover is completely forgotten as I rush back down the hallway, poking my head into Bishop and Vee's small room as I go. Bishop was right. Her gun is nowhere to be seen, but her bag is right where she left it by the wall.

I continue on until I reach the front of the building, where Warren is clutching his head and popping painkillers from the blister pack I left on the floor. "Man, that stuff's brutal." He nods towards the spilled Lagavulin in the floor. "I'm sticking to beer from now on, even if I can't find a cold one." He looks up at me with bloodshot eyes. "Jesus, what happened?"

I look down at my bloody shirt and wave it away. "Doesn't matter. Vee's been taken. Some guy came in the night and knocked Bishop out. She's gone, but her stuff's still here."

Warren's face turns gray as I speak, and his eyes flit guiltily to the empty bottle on the floor. "Jesus, I should have been awake."

"We can blame ourselves later," I say, grabbing my jacket and checking the gun is still there. "For now let's just concentrate on getting her back."

Warren nods, hefts his rifle from the windowsill and scoops his stuff into his duffel bag before following me out the door. Along the way we find Bishop moping in the hallway, and after grabbing Vee's bag the three of us move quietly down through the building, checking along the way that we're alone.

It's only when we reach the ground floor that we realize how fucked we really are. Through the propped open glass door I see a dozen infected milling in the street... and one of them is standing in the empty spot where we parked the car.

"I don't suppose you have a spare vehicle in that duffel, Warren?" I nod out the door to the empty space.

Warren looks out, and when he turns back I can see he's smiling. "No, I don't," he says, rooting through Vee's bag, "but I do have a homing beacon." He pulls out a chunky black device that looks like an iPhone and a walkie talkie had a kid. "Sat phone," he says, clicking the thick, stumpy rubber antenna into place. "My battery died last week, but

Vee still has a bit of charge. Aaaaaaand..."
He taps the screen a couple times, frowning.
"Yep, here it is. Big mistake, you dumb
bastard. Karl's phone was still in the trunk
with the rest of his stuff." He flips the phone
around, and I can see a blue dot flashing on
the screen against a faint map. It's moving
west along what looks like Highway 78.

"OK, shut it down." I point to the red
battery warning in the corner. "Save the
power. We can power it back up when we
have a car. Speaking of which, any idea how
we're gonna get past these guys outside?"

Warren shrugs the rifle off his shoulder.
"How do you think? You know how to turn
your safety off?"

I slip the Beretta from my jacket pocket
and flip the catch with my thumb. "Got it.
Bishop, get ready to hold this door when we
shout, OK? Warren, I'll give you backup
from here. Try to keep it quiet."

Bishop nods, and Warren sees what I'm
getting at. He takes a knee by the door and
checks his gun while I take up position just

behind him. "Good thinking, kid. We'll make a soldier of you yet."

Six of the dozen are on the ground before the first of them notices us. Warren's rifle reports echo through the street and the infected swing around wildly, hunting for the source of the sound as their brothers drop to the deck. Once one of them notices us, though, it only takes a few seconds for the rest to pick it up and come charging in.

It's been almost a decade since I last fired a gun. I'd forgotten how the noise fills your entire world when the gun is only at arm's length, but I don't flinch. I hold it steady and squeeze off rounds until the magazine runs empty and the slide springs back, and by the time I'm squeezing the trigger on air there are four more infected down.

The final two are just a few yards away now. I'm empty and Warren can't seem to slide the bolt forward on his M40. I barely hear him yell above the ringing in my ears, but Bishop barrels forward from behind us and wedges himself against the door at the very moment the two crash into it. The door rattles in its frame and a spiderweb appears in the toughened glass, but it doesn't shatter.

"Hold the door!" I yell, releasing my magazine to the ground before I slot the fresh one in. I feel the click as it seats, pull back the slide and step forward, nodding at Bishop to move aside. He wedges his foot against the door, relaxes his shoulder a little and gives me a couple inches space. The sound of the Beretta firing through the gap in the door is deafening. Bishop flinches and steps away, allowing it to swing open, but the two infected are already down.

My hands are shaking and I feel lightheaded, looking down at the dozen bodies lying in the street before us. Most of them look like they've been infected a while. They're thin and sinewy, their clothes ragged and dirty, but the final two - the two I shot at close range - look like they only turned recently. One of them looks to be a teenage boy, maybe sixteen or so.

I'm still staring down at the kid when Warren takes the Beretta from my hand, pulls back the slide to check the chamber, and calmly puts a bullet in his head. "You only winged him," he says. "Gotta watch out for that. Other than that, pretty solid performance for your first time." He looks around at the carnage and nods with approval. "OK, let's start checking cars. Every infected for a mile heard that racket, and I don't wanna be around when they come for a look see."

Roy winces in the driver's seat, shifting uncomfortably and choking back panicked tears. Just an hour ago he felt like he was on the verge of his greatest triumph. He'd have a hot piece of ass tied up in the back of his new car, he'd be on the way back to safety at the community, and if the mood struck he'd pull over and break in that cute Latino bitch before sharing her around.

All that happened as planned, but if he could go back and do it again he'd walk back to his shitty wreck of a car, gun the engine and get the hell out of there. No piece of ass is worth this much pain. Even the safety of the community isn't worth what's happening in his pants.

The bitch kicked him. Hard. She woke at the sound of Roy's gun clocking out the big guy, and she kicked out before he even realized she had her eyes open. The thick, heavy heel of her dumbass army boots crushed his left testicle against his pelvic bone - he was probably imagining it, but he'd swear he heard it burst - and then she dragged her foot down his thigh and did all sorts of damage to his cock.

He looks down at his open pants and starts gibbering frantically. It's... it's just a fucking mess. His left ball is swollen up like a hard boiled egg. His scrotum is stretched tight as a drum, and he can't even hold his legs closed for fear that the lightest brush against his skin will result in fresh waves of agony. As for his cock... Jesus, it looks like someone took a belt sander to it. A roll of torn skin hangs loose, and the blood gushing from the wound has glued it like a Post-It note to his right thigh.

He doesn't dare touch anything. The pain didn't kick in until after he'd knocked her out with the butt of the gun, but as soon as the message from his groin reached his brain he almost puked from the agony. It was all he could do to drag her down to the car without passing out. He'd almost killed her there and then, but just before he gave in to his rage and put his last two bullets in her skull he had a rare attack of common sense. He realized he'd need a doctor if he was ever going to be able to fuck again, and the only doc he knew lived at the community.

Fighting the strongest urge to slaughter the bitch he tied her up, bundled her into the trunk of the Toyota and painfully eased into the driver's seat.

Roy looks down again and begins to weep as he sees a trickle of blood pour from his pee hole. He's no doctor, but he knows that ain't good. Blood from there means he's all torn up inside. This isn't a wound that'll be right as rain after just a few stitches. This means surgery. Anesthesia. Pain drugs. Bed rest. He's pretty sure they'll let him back in with the girl, but will one piece of pussy be enough to earn him a month of the doc's time? It's touch and go.

By the time he sees the sign for Harrisburg he feels cold and weak, and in the rear view mirror his face looks drawn and pale. He can't tell how much blood he's already lost, but the seat beneath his ass is soaking wet and ice cold. He glances down and starts to shake when he sees the torn skin on his cock looks dusky, and his swollen left nut has started to turn a terrifying shade of purple. He doesn't even want to guess what that means, but an unpleasant word has been rattling around his mind for the last forty miles: amputation.

The end of the world didn't faze Roy at all. He'd never had anything to begin with, so he had nothing to lose. All the collapse of society had done was drag everyone back down to his level, and Roy counted that as a win. Roy, 1. World, 0. This, though... this thing between his legs, it's the one thing that didn't cost anything. The one thing the government couldn't tax, the one thing that brought him joy, and that bitch in the trunk tried to take it away from him.

As soon as he recovers he'll make her pay for every bit of the pain she's caused, punch by punch. Once he's done with her she'll beg him to kill her, but he won't give her the relief. He'll ruin her, and then he'll shove her broken body out into the street for the infected to play with.

Finally he reaches the Harrisburg exit, and he almost smiles as he pulls the car into the city and heads down the familiar streets towards the community. The pain has begun to radiate down his left leg, and he can tell he won't last much longer without medical attention. The doc had better be awake and sober.

A road flare spins a few times in the air before landing on the street about fifty yards ahead of him, spitting out a stream of red sparks. He slows, approaching the blockade carefully. He knows they don't have any problem opening fire on strangers, but he knows they usually wait until they establish whether a new arrival is a threat before taking aim. He drops his speed to a crawl and flashes his lights, waving slowly out the window. He almost weeps with relief when they wave him in closer, and then his blood runs cold when he sees the guard's expression harden as he recognizes Roy. He turns the car around and carefully backs up as close as he dares, just in case they decide to start shooting.

"Hell no. Head right back the way you came, Roy. You know you're not welcome here." The guard hikes up his rifle and points it down from his perch on top of the blockade.

"*Woah, woah, woah*, it ain't like before," Roy pleads, pushing open the door. "I brought a... a, a peace offering for you guys. Trust me, you're gonna love it." He climbs out of the car, remembering too late that his pants are still unzipped and the mess of his crotch is on display. The guard turns away in disgust. "Never mind that. I just had a bit of trouble on the way, the doc'll fix me right up. Now look what I brought you guys." He limps slowly to the back of the car and pops the trunk, and the guard breaks into a cautious smile when he sees what's inside.

Vee lies on her side, her legs tightly bound at the knees and feet, her arms strapped painfully behind her back. Her mouth is bound with Roy's jean jacket, one of the arms pushed between her lips and tied around the back of her head. She bucks and struggles, but Roy knows how to tie a solid knot. It'd take days for her to work her way free, and she only woke up a half hour ago.

Roy looks up at the guard and nods towards the rusted yellow school bus blocking the blockade entrance. "So... you think we might be able to deal?"

The guard doesn't speak. He just looks behind him, waves a hand and vanishes from sight. Moments later the school bus begins to silently move, dragged backwards by some unseen pulley system until there's just enough room for the Toyota to pull through the gap. Several armed men pour like soldier ants through the opening, taking up defensive positions as Roy carefully climbs back into the car and reverses through the gap. They stay vigilant, watching for infected until the car is safely through, then as one they withdraw to safety, training their weapons on the opening until the moment the bus returns to block the way.

Nothing breaches the walls of the community. In the old days it was the most exclusive hotel in the city. $200 would buy you a night in one of its cheapest beds. Today, though, the price is much higher. If you want to live within the secure walls of the Harrisburg Hilton you'll need to pledge your life to the Chief.

Warren looks up from his scope. "Absolute tactical shit for brains. Damn idiot civilians can't do anything right." He looks over at me. "Sorry, no offense, Tom. It's just... I mean, Jesus H Christ, what kind of idiot sets up a defensive position in a building at a damned four way intersection? And how dumb do you have to be to leave all the tall buildings around you unprotected? It's amateur hour in Harrisburg."

It's hard to argue with Warren's assessment. We're sitting beside our stolen ambulance on the sixth floor of the Market Square garage, across the street from the Crowne Plaza Hotel and just two blocks from the location of Warren's homing beacon. I can see the obvious weaknesses in the compound's defenses. I don't have the first clue about military tactics, but I know we can see - and could fire, if we wanted to - into every window on the front of the building. We might not have a clear shot into any of the rooms at this angle, but we could give everyone inside a damned good fright.

The Harrisburg Hilton seems to be the only building in the compound. We slowly coasted a few blocks around it as we arrived in the city, and by the looks of it there are strong, well defended blockades built from wrecked cars on each of the roads around the building, with guards stationed on walkways at the top of each one. It seems like it'd be nigh on impossible to breach the place by road without being cut down by the guards, but the compound is hardly airtight. The Hilton is surrounded on three sides by buildings that loom over it, and apart from having the doors bricked up they're all easily accessible to anyone who really wanted to get in.

"I could take out most of the guards from right here," Warren mutters, sighting down his scope, his finger well clear of the trigger. I can see four atop the two blockades visible from the garage, all dressed in civilian clothing and carrying a random assortment of guns. From the vantage point of the garage even I could probably take them out myself before they made it back across the open ground to the hotel. It really doesn't seem like a secure site.

"Is that the plan?" I ask, suddenly nervous.

Warren shakes his head. "Waste of ammo. We came across a couple of places like this in the last few weeks. Damn things started popping up everywhere soon as the cops pulled out." He sighs and pulls his rifle back over the edge. "They're damn near all run by dumbass survivalists who think they're playing some kind of video game. Not your hardcore guys, mind you. The real hardcore survivalists had their bunkers ready and waiting years ago. These guys are your part timers. Weekend warriors, y'know? They subscribe to the magazines, but they're mostly just losers who couldn't hack it in the real world." He peers over the edge. "They're well provisioned, though, and if they're anything like the others we've seen they'll have enough guns and ammo to take out a small country. Nah, a full frontal assault won't do us any good against these particular assholes. We just don't have the numbers."

A shot rings out without warning from the nearest blockade, echoing down the street. We both duck our heads beneath the wall and prepare for more. For a moment I can only hear the sound of my own heart beating in my throat, each pulse as loud as a shot, but nothing comes. It's thirty seconds before I finally dare raise my head, and almost immediately another shot blasts out, its echo bouncing off the walls of the tall buildings surrounding us. For the first time I consider that we didn't plan our escape from the garage, and as far as I know there's only a single exit. If the compound sends out scouts to find us we'll be sitting ducks.

As I glance over the wall and down to the street, though, I catch something out of the corner of my eye before I duck back down. Six floors below us a small group of infected wander towards the blockade, seemingly unaware that they're drifting towards death. From the top of the blockade a guard rests his rifle on the roof of a pickup, carefully sighting through his scope before taking potshots at the creatures. I raise my head again, and even from this distance I can see that his gun is trained on the street and not us. Another shot comes, a woman falls to the ground as if her legs have been swept out from under her, and the seed of a plan begins to form in my mind.

"Warren," I whisper, nodding down to the doomed herd beneath us, "what kind of numbers do you think we need?"

Vee spits the taste of Roy's musky sweat from her mouth the moment the denim gag leaves her mouth, and she struggles for a moment to hold back the vomit until she can finally take a deep breath.

"I'll fucking kill you," she gasps, straining against the ropes binding her arms and legs. "Let me the fuck out of here, now!"

The man looming over her holds up his hands to calm her, reaching down to her ankles to loosen the straps. "Please, please, ma'am, don't struggle. We mean you no harm." He quickly moves away from her legs as her ankles work loose from the rope, avoiding the flailing kick she telegraphed from a mile away. "Please, you have to believe me, I don't mean to hurt you." He carefully tugs loose the knot between her wrists and takes a few quick steps back as she finally frees herself.

Vee rolls herself off the bed quickly, backing into the corner and scanning the room as her captor cowers away. It looks like some kind of hotel room; comfortable but sterile, without any obvious weapons within reaching distance. "Why the fuck did you take me prisoner?"

The man lets out a soft chuckle and shakes his head. "I didn't. I can only apologize, ma'am, on behalf of Roy. He was one of our less... disciplined residents. We didn't quite see eye to eye on a number of subjects, and we had no choice but to exile him after it became clear he didn't fit in with our little community." He looks behind him as the back of his knees hit a stool, and he calmly takes a seat. "I'm afraid Roy somehow got it into his head that we'd welcome him back with open arms if he brought us a peace offering, and I'm sorry to say that he intended you to be that offering. I'm so sorry for everything that's happened to you. Please... I assure you I'm not your enemy."

Vee feels the injured rage begin to drain from her, a sensation she doesn't really appreciate. She's happy to learn that her situation may not be as dire as she feared, but she feels a little cheated that she won't get the chance to have her revenge right away. She's been dreaming of that perfect punch since the moment she woke up in the trunk of the car, and the urge to throw it anyway is almost overwhelming.

Still... she can't deny that there's something oddly comforting about the man before her. Despite his quick, fearful withdrawal as he loosened her ropes it's clear he's in command here. There's something about the relaxed way he sits on the little beige stool by the dressing table that tells her he owns this room. Hell, he seems like he'd own every room he walked into. He seems so... so confident. Self-possessed. If she didn't know better she'd say he was accustomed to command. Military, maybe?

He's even a little good looking, she realizes. Well built. A little gray in his cropped dark hair. Old enough to look a little rough around the edges, but young enough to retain the sort of boyish looks that let Patrick Dempsey walk into a few roles his acting skills didn't warrant.

"Don't forget that I favor my left leg." he says, smiling. "An old war wound? A memento from a bar fight? Childhood polio?"

Vee blushes as she realizes he can read her just as well as she can read him. "Old habit."

He chuckles and lifts himself to his feet. "Don't worry about it, I size up everyone I meet, too. Doesn't matter, though. The old rules don't mean anything any more. You think you can do a Sherlock Holmes and figure out that I'm a high school math teacher because I have a chalk mark on my sleeve and my loafers haven't been polished for three weeks?" He slips out a full pack of cigarettes and runs his thumb around the foil until he finds the break. "Couple weeks back I met a math teacher with four dozen kills to his name. Day after that I saw a Marine so scared he put a bullet in the roof of his mouth." He finally tears the foil from the pack, opens it up and then reconsiders. "I don't think you can judge a book by its cover any more."

Vee smiles for the first time. She pats her pockets for her own cigarettes, finds she's been stripped of her belongings and happily accepts the tossed pack from the man. "Thanks. I'm Victoria. What do I call you?"

He smiles. "Call me the Chief." He sees Vee about to open her mouth and cuts her off. "Yeah, just the Chief. I'm ex-military, like you probably guessed. If this shit ever comes good and we get back to some semblance of normal I don't want my name dragged through the mud, you know? It'd be nice if I could just slip quietly out the back door, head back to base and pretend none of this ever happened. I don't think my superiors would be all that thrilled to learn I abandoned my post and started up my own little kingdom,"

Vee laughs as she lights her cigarette. "You and me both. I called it a day a little more than a week ago, but I doubt I'd ever go back even if everything went back to normal tomorrow morning. Too many bad memories. If I get through this I'm looking for a fresh start." Something occurs to her. "So, what happened to the guy who brought me here? I want to spend a little alone time with him, if it's OK with you. He needs to be taught a lesson, and I'm eager to teach it."

The Chief smiles and shakes his head. "I wish I could help, but that isn't the way we do things here. We don't kill within our walls. Our only punishment is exile, but as I understand you already inflicted injuries that will amount to the same thing once he leaves our protection. In fact..." He stands and strolls over to the window. "Yes, there he is. If you'd like to watch?"

Vee cautiously walks towards the window as the Chief raises his walkie talkie. "Yeah, it's me," he says. "Send the fucker out."

Vee looks out the window and sees she's a couple of floors above street level. She's looking down on the front of the building where an area has been cleared between the high roadblocks penning in the compound. A dozen or so armed men loiter in the street, and as she watches one of them breaks from the pack, walks towards the front door and, a moment later, returns dragging a struggling man. Even from four floors up she can tell it's Roy. He limps and struggles with the wounds she inflicted with her boot, and he clearly lacks the strength to put up a fight.

Another guard walks around to the back of the beat up yellow school bus that serves as the gate for the largest roadblock. He grabs a couple of loose cables, hooks them up to a car battery sitting on the ground and hits a button that starts an electric winch, tugging a cable taut and pulling the bus back until there's just enough room for a man to fit through the gap.

The Chief pushes open the window, and suddenly she can hear Roy's weeping and pleading. From this distance she can't make out the words, but it's clear he's begging the guards to let him stay. They don't respond. They barely even look at him. The guard who pulled him from the building simply drags him to the opening like a disobedient child, and unceremoniously shoves him out onto the street beyond the road block before a group of guards push the school bus forward until the gap is closed.

Now Roy seems insensible. He drops to the ground and tries to slide under the bus, but it becomes clear when he reemerges that there's something blocking the way. He then tries to climb the cars, but after just a few moments he falls back, exhausted and crying with pain. The front of his jeans are stained dark with blood, and even his hands are red with it.

A guard climbs slowly to the top of the roadblock, and for a moment he calmly surveys the street into the distance until he finds what he's searching for. About two hundred yards down the road a small group of infected mill around aimlessly, seemingly unaware of the presence of the living at the other end of the street. The guard slips two fingers between his lips and lets out a shrill, loud whistle, and immediately the infected snap up their heads and hunt for the source of the sound.

Vee feels her stomach turn over as they begin to run. There are four of them, all in the late stages as far as she can tell from this distance. They're too far gone to manage a full sprint, but their speed doesn't matter at this point. Roy is blocked in on all sides: the roadblock behind him, boarded up buildings to either side and the infected shambling towards him from ahead. Maybe if he was at full strength he'd have a chance of evading them, but it's clear he couldn't fight off a cold right now.

Now the group are just a hundred yards away, and Vee catches the sound of their snarls on the breeze. Inhuman. Hungry.

Desperate. They look emaciated, like they haven't eaten in weeks, and they couldn't be more eager to help themselves to an easy meal.

"Stop this," she says, grabbing the Chief by the arm. "Nobody should have to die like that." She's as surprised as anyone by her words. She'd happily kill Roy by her own hand if she had the chance. She's put a bullet in his skull without a shred of guilt, but this is different. This isn't just execution. This is torture.

The Chief shrugs her off and concentrates on the scene below. "We have rules, Victoria. Roy broke those rules, and now he has to pay the price." He turns to her, and she's shocked to see that every scrap of the friendly, charming man she'd seen just a moment ago has vanished, replaced by something else. Something cold and calculating, almost reptilian. "I told him not to come back. This is what happens when my people disobey me."

The Chief is *enjoying* this.

The infected are just a few steps away now. Vee desperately wants to turn away but she just can't. Her eyes are locked on the scene, and she can't help but imagine her husband standing there as teeth tore into his flesh. She can't help but remember every one of her friends taken by the infected over the last hellish month. She can't turn away, and she can't close her eyes.

Roy falls to his knees, weeping and resigned to his fate. He doesn't even try to run. He knows there's no hope as the infected close in.

The first one reaches him now. It's a young man dressed in the torn, dirty rags of an oversized gray suit. He looks to be about eighteen years old. Boyish and fresh faced, probably on the way to his first real job when the infection took hold. He's missing his left arm up to the shoulder, but a spur of bone around eight inches long still remains. As he descends on Roy the bone swings around like a phantom limb, as if the boy isn't aware that the arm is no longer there and still tries to punch with it.

He's clumsy and uncoordinated, and when the second member of the group, an older woman completely naked and missing chunks of flesh from her torso, barrels into him from behind he tumbles forward onto Roy. The boy tries to steady himself with the missing arm, and as he falls the sharp spur of bone pierces Roy's stomach and vanishes inside his body. Roy lets out a piercing scream and tries to struggle away, but as he scrambles backwards the bone simply tears his midriff open wider. The final two infected reach him now, and they see his ripped open stomach as nothing but a buffet.

Vee feels bile rise to her throat as all four infected reach into Roy's body and begin to pull their share of his intestines out to feast. They drag the slippery pink tubes to their mouths, ignoring Roy's weak screams and kicking legs as they chew into the rubbery mass. They squabble over him, each of them jealously guarding their meal from the others. Each of them grab the offal from each other's hands, pulling it away, dragging more and more from Roy's body until the asphalt around him is swimming in blood, flesh and half digested slurry.

Still Roy is alive. Still he weakly cries out with agony, his eyes wide open and staring in horror at the glistening offal that spills from him. He holds out a weak hand to push his attackers away, but the youngest boy simply grabs the hand by the wrist and bites down on a finger, gnawing through the flesh until he reaches the bone.

Vee finally manages to tear her eyes away from the scene, her legs weak and her stomach turning, but the Chief continues to stare, smiling until one of the infected finally reaches deep within Roy's chest cavity and tugs until the wet, pink mass of a lung tears from his body. Finally his cries stop, and the only sounds that remain are the snarls of the dead and the moist slurping of their feast.

Vee steadies herself against the wall and flinches as five silenced shots ring out. She turns back to see the infected fall to the ground, their mouths still full of Roy. The fifth shot obliterated Roy's face, ensuring that he won't return to take his vengeance on the guards.

The Chief nods with satisfaction, turns on his heel and makes his way towards the door as Vee stares down at the pile of bodies beyond the roadblock. "You'll be happy here with us, Victoria. The women here are... quite comfortable, so long as they understand their role. I'm sure you understand that I can't release you now you've seen our operation, not now I know you're military." He stops at the door, and places his hand on the butt of the gun holstered at his waist when he sees Vee take a step towards him. She stops. "And if we can't make you happy, well..." He leaves the sentence hanging in the air.

"Rest up now. I'll have some food sent up for you shortly, and then you can start work." He looks her up and down with cold eyes. "We have a lot of men here I'm sure are eager to make your acquaintance."

Bishop's sweaty hands slip on the steering wheel, he's so nervous as the ambulance cruises slowly through the streets of Harrisburg. Warren sits beside him calling out directions as we approach each intersection, and I sit in the back and look out the open door at the growing crowd of infected giving chase.

"A little faster," I call out, nervously gripping the Beretta as one of them comes within ten paces of the vehicle. I just pray we don't reach a blockage in the road. If we have to stop for any reason a swarm of infected will flood into the back of the ambulance, and my clever little plan with be the last I ever make.

"Coming up on a big herd," Warren calls out from the front. "Bishop, give it a little gas." The ambulance jerks as it speeds up, and as we drive beside a large open square I feel myself shiver at the sight of scores of infected locking onto our movement and launching themselves into a run. They follow us like the tail of a comet, dragging behind us for a hundred yards as we crawl through the streets just a little too quickly for them to catch up. It's a chilling sight.

I feel my heart thump in my chest as I recognize the street we're on. We're almost back at the garage now. Just a few hundred more yards and it'll be game time. Either the plan will work perfectly or we'll be trapped with no escape as hundreds of infected tear us to pieces.

In the passenger seat Warren grips the bipod he uses for his rifle, extending the telescopic legs until they reach the required length. He'll have to judge the distance right, or he'll still be fiddling with it as the dead catch us.

"OK, you guys ready?" he calls out. I nod, and Bishop simply grips the steering wheel tighter. "You ready, Bishop?" Finally he nods and speeds up until there's a hundred yards or so between the ambulance and the quickest of the swarm. That should be enough to keep them chasing, but it should also be enough to give us the time to work before they catch us.

Bishop turns the corner at speed, and for a moment it feels as if the vehicle lifts onto two wheels as we jerkily skid onto the street running towards the largest roadblock. Warren rests his hand on Bishop's shoulder to calm him, and when he finally pulls to a halt he jumps out of the ambulance as if it's on fire. I do the same, leaping out of the back and sprinting with Bishop to the dark entrance of the parking garage, while Warren tugs on the emergency brake and jams the legs of the bipod between the frame of the driver's seat and the gas pedal, pinning it to the ground. The engine lets out a tortured whine as the revs build up, and moments later Warren releases the brake and leaps out of the vehicle as it begins to move.

It's already three car lengths away by the time Warren reaches the garage, and moments after he rolls behind a low wall to conceal himself the first of the infected races around the corner, spots the accelerating ambulance and tears towards it. The rest of the swarm quickly follows. Hundreds of them pour around the corner and continue on, and none of us dare watch in case they notice us hiding.

For a long, painful moment I hold my breath and squeeze my eyes closed, terrified that the mad thumping of my heart would kill me stone dead there and then as hundreds of stinking infected swarm by just a few yards away on the other side of the wall. I flinch when I hear gunshots, and after twenty seconds I finally dare poke my head over the wall to see what's happening.

The last of the swarm has passed us. In the distance the ambulance continues to accelerate towards the roadblock, veering a little off course with torque steer but still pointed in the right direction. I can hear the panicked yells of the guards as they fire wildly at the front window of the ambulance, presumably trying to kill a driver who isn't there. Bullets ricochet from the vehicle, but it plows on regardless.

The ambulance hits the school bus at speed, striking it close to the back and shunting the rear wheels ten feet to the right before the engine finally dies and the power fades. It's more than enough. A wide gap has opened in the roadblock, and within just a few moments the swarm of infected reach it at a dead sprint.

The guards are in disarray. A dozen or so hide out at the top of the barriers and fire down into the swarm, but they may as well be firing into water. For every infected they put down three more replace them, and it isn't long before the strongest of them begin to climb the wrecked cars until they reach the terrified living.

We waste no time now the guards are too busy being eaten to notice us. Bishop, Warren and I sprint as fast as we can across the empty street on what's now the 'safe' side of the largest roadblock, and when we reach it we take a right and quickly climb to the top of the secondary barrier blocking the road the runs along the side wall of the hotel. This one isn't manned, but beyond it in the empty no man's land lies a service entrance and a delivery bay, its rolling shutter wide open and unguarded.

Warren leads the way, his rifle slung over his shoulder and his pistol clutched in one hand. In the other he holds his sat phone, its battery indicator blinking warning flashes but still carrying enough juice to show us the location of its twin. With a little luck it will lead us to Vee, and we can all get the fuck out of here.

"Should be just up ahead," Warren whispers, stepping through a door beside the delivery bay that leads into a large storage room filled to the ceiling with sheets, towels, bathrobes and anything else fluffy and white enough to proudly carry the Hilton name. We sneak through the aisles with our guns raised, stepping carefully to avoid making too much of a noise on the tile floor, until we reach the far wall and realize the room is empty.

Almost empty, anyway. Propped against a stack of towels lies an M16, and beside it a small duffel bag. Warren takes a knee beside it and fumbles within until he pulls out a boxy sat phone. "This is Karl's bag," he sighs, dropping the phone back inside. "They must have brought in everything from the trunk. But where the fuck did they take Vee?"

Bishop points to a door hidden between two aisles. "Maybe she's through there," he suggests, stepping towards it. Before Warren can warn him to stop he tugs it open, and beyond its frame the world is going to hell.

"Bar the doors, now!" comes a panicked voice followed by an unintelligible protest. "Because I fucking said so! They're already dead! Now bar the fucking door!"

I creep to the door and look out on what I immediately realize is the hotel lobby. The storage room opens behind the concierge desk, and across the wide, airy room a dozen or more men struggle to lock down the revolving door at the front of the building. They try to slot a locking pin into the marble floor to prevent the door from turning, but they can't seem to get it in. I creep out a little further and hide behind the desk, and I can see why right away.

A crowd of infected force themselves against one of the panes of glass in the door, desperately trying to push their way through. Just ahead of them in the section of the door sealed closed stands a man. Alive, and armed with a pistol. Through the glass I hear him plead to the men on the inside to let him in, but they just continue to struggle with the lock. They know that if they allow the guard to enter they'll only be a single pane between them and the infected, and it looks like they're willing to sacrifice their friend for the sake of that extra pane.

I turn back to the storage room and beckon Warren and Bishop closer. "Come on, while they're distracted." They both drop into a crouch and run behind the desk, then Warren silently points towards the staircase to the left of the lobby and makes his move. We both follow.

As we reach the foot of the stairs I hear a single gunshot. I drop to the ground and freeze, but no more shots come. It's only when I hear the voice that I realize that the shot wasn't intended for me.

"You fucking asshole, you shot Josh!"

I turn in time to see the man trapped within the revolving door slump against the glass and slide to the ground. A guard kitted out in bulky riot gear pulls back his pistol from the narrow gap in the door and holsters it. "Better him than us," he says, turning away. "If we'd let him in the rest would be inside soon enough. Now you, you, you," he points to three guys in the group. "Get upstairs and start picking those fuckers off from the windows before they break through."

The three chosen men nod and turn towards the staircase. Towards us.

I move with a speed I didn't know I possessed until I'm hidden behind a wide marble column, and as the men reach the staircase and leap up two steps at a time I realize Warren and Bishop are no longer there. I can't see where they went, but they must have run as soon as they heard the shot.

For a moment I stand with my back pressed against the column, unsure what the hell I should be doing, but eventually I figure there's no going back. The men still in the lobby will eventually head this way, and if they're willing to shoot one of their own without a second thought I don't want to find out what they'd do to me. Up ahead at the top of the flight I see a sign: an arrow pointing to the left, followed by room numbers. Just to the right of it hangs an emergency map with the locations of the fire exits. If I can't get out the way I came maybe there's another route that's less crowded with armed guards and the dead.

I take a deep breath, tighten my grip on the Beretta and push myself away from the column, bounding up the stairs as fast as I can. I don't breathe again until I round the corner and find myself at the beginning of a long, empty corridor, flanked on both sides with an endless row of doors.

Vee stands by the window, looking out over the compound and trying to formulate a plan. Down at street level the area behind the roadblocks is packed with guards, almost all of them armed, and she has a clear view down three of the four streets leading away from the hotel. They're all free of obstacles with a clear line of sight off into the distance. Even if she could somehow find a way to climb down from the open window there's no way she'd ever make it to safety without being picked off. It'd be like shooting fish in a barrel for the guards armed with sniper rifles.

No, there has to be another way. but she's damned if she can see it. The Chief locked the door securely on his way out, and unless she wants to try to overpower the next person to come through the door - unarmed, at that - she's not getting out through there either.

She's staring back at the locked door when she hears a commotion through the window. Panicked yelling, shouted orders and the sharp rattle of automatic gunfire. She rushes back just in time to see the school bus jump to the side, forced out of the way by a speeding ambulance plowing into its side. Her blood runs cold as she sees what's running behind it. Hundreds of infected catch up with the ambulance as its ruined radiator vents steam against the side of the crushed bus. Some swarm over it, fighting to get at whoever was inside, while many more flood through the gap and into the compound. The first few fall as a hail of bullets tears through their bodies, but for every one that falls many more swarm through. There aren't enough guards to take them down quickly enough. They weren't prepared, and it's only moments before the first falls in a mass of grabbing hands and biting teeth. She turns away with a look of disgust as a young boy dips down towards the struggling guard's face, moments later coming back up with an eye between his teeth, still attached to the screaming guard by a length of wet, stringy flesh.

Vee turns away and scans the room urgently as the swarm begins to turn to the front door of the building. If they're coming inside there's no way she'll allow herself to stay trapped in a locked room until they take her. *Never infected.* That was the rule. If she dies, she dies fucking fighting.

"Think, Victoria, *think*," she whispers to herself as she surveys the room. It's pretty basic, just a simple double bed and a small dressing table at its foot. There's nothing solid enough to even consider attempting to break open the door. She stalks through to the small bathroom, and immediately an idea hits her. The lid of the toilet cistern looks heavy enough to use to destroy the door handle. Maybe - just maybe - if she hits it hard enough she can loosen the lock and manage to open the door.

She grabs the heavy lid, rushes back to the door, raises the thick porcelain above her head and brings it down with all her power onto the brushed steel handle. The porcelain shatters into a dozen pieces with the force of the blow and Vee staggers backwards, flinching away and raising her arm to protect herself from the flying shards.

She opens her eyes and lowers her arm.

Nothing. The handle is still there, barely even scratched by the shattering porcelain.

Fuck.

She refuses to give up, rushing back into the bathroom to come up with plan B. *Maybe... maybe... ah, there it is.*

She climbs onto the lip of the bathtub and grabs at the long steel shower rod, lowering herself down to test its strength against her weight. Maybe she'll be able to use it as a support to shimmy across the gap between her window and one of the rooms to either side. It's a long shot, but it's better than waiting here to die.

She braces herself against the wall, plants her feet firmly on the edge of the tub and pushes up with all her strength, forcing the the rod to break away from the bolt securing it to the tile wall. It moves a little but doesn't break, so she pulls down with all her weight before pushing once again. The tile around the rod begins to crack, and she blinks dust from her eyes as the rod begins to loosen from its mooring.

With a final firm push the rod is freed, and without any more resistance it shoots up towards the ceiling. Thick clouds of white dust shower down onto her, and she slips from the lip of the tub and cracks her head on the basin as she falls. The pain is intense, and she fights to remain conscious as a ringing builds in her ears and her vision grows muddy with colored spots, dust and tears.

After a few moments she shakes her head and forces herself to her feet. She feels a trickle of blood run down the back of her neck, but there's no time to worry about that right now. She climbs back onto the edge of the tub, reaches out to grab the freed rod, looks up and...

And her lips spread in a broad grin.

"Thank God for cost cutting," she whispers to herself, smiling up at the ceiling. When the rod came loose it pushed against the plain white ceiling she'd assumed was solid and unbreakable, but now she looks up and sees a wide hole broken through cheap half inch sheet rock that even now crumbles around the edges. In the darkness above she can see wooden support beams set wide enough to climb between, and beyond them the dim glow of lights that must be coming from the hallway on the other side of the wall.

With the shower rod to help she makes quick work of widening the hole, and after just a few moments she grabs a beam in each hand and lifts herself into the dark crawlspace above. In the half light she crawls on hands and knees until she reaches the beam that marks the edge of the room. She climbs over, clenches her fists into a ball and pounds down on the sheet rock beneath her until it collapses. The crawlspace floods with light from the hallway below, and she grabs a beam and easily lowers herself to freedom.

"Vee!" A surprised voice cries out behind her.

Jacob Moore stands with his back pressed against the concierge desk, praying for the others to return while there's still time. Everyone else ran upstairs to take potshots at the infected from above, leaving him alone with nothing to protect himself but his dad's old Mossberg 500 shotgun. He stares through the revolving door with wide, tear filled eyes at the swarm of infected still beating against the glass, and at one in particular: his dad.

Jacob had been due to go on guard duty with his father. He should have been out there, but he'd been caught short and rushed off to the bathroom just ten minutes before the swarm breached the perimeter. He'd watched through the glass as a group of them had descended on his dad, and his feet had been frozen to the ground as he watched them crack his bones until his arms hung loose in their sockets. As one of them leaned down and clamped its jaws over his dad's face he'd felt the warmth spread in his pants, but still he'd been unable to move. Even if he could have gotten through the door to save him he'd have been powerless. He was frozen with fear, and now that fear was multiplied beyond counting.

His dad's face is contorted with rage, barely recognizable as he pounds madly against the glass. His right cheek is missing, and his dentures have slipped so far to the side that they're almost falling out of the gap. Blood gushes down his dirty white shirt, drooling down his chin and spraying against the bulging window as he yells wordlessly.

The glass is breaking under the weight of the infected. With each pounding fist it shatters a little more, the tiny fractures spreading ever closer to the frame. Jacob knows that at any moment the whole door will shatter, and once that happens he's dead. There's no way he can take out more than a couple with the two 00 buckshot shells in the Mossberg.

He also know he can't fire on his father. He can't fire on the man who saved him when his mother turned; the man who dragged him to the car and gunned the engine until they were far away from the house... far away from the bodies of his mother, brother and sisters.

He knows his dad's gone. He's scared, but he's not stupid. He knows the creature pounding at the glass isn't really his old man any more. Even so, even as the window bulges in just a little more he knows he won't be able to pull the trigger. He won't be able to fire, knowing that the shot will take away the last member of his family.

He closes his eyes when he hears the glass finally give way. He squeezes them tight when he hears the groans and pants of the infected, and swings the shotgun around as he hears their footfalls on the tile. The barrel slips awkwardly between his lips, chipping a tooth in his haste, but he ignores the pain. He reaches down and his fingers hunt for the trigger. His thumb closes over it, and he pulls down while holding the barrel steady against the roof of his mouth with his tongue.

He isn't fast enough. His attacker knocks his hand away from the trigger before he can fire, and he loses his grip on the gun as he's pushed backwards over the concierge desk. He falls to the ground, his eyes open, and looming above him he sees his father, bloodstained and wild eyed, lunge down towards him with clenched fists.

The boy stays conscious for... who knows how long? Nobody alive is there to see it, and nobody alive cares about his pain. He feels every blow. Every bite. He feels it as his father gouges his left eye deep into his skull with his thumb. He feels his own eyeball burst, and his mouth opens in a silent scream until the pain is so great he slips away.

There's no more pain. He doesn't feel the punches any more. He doesn't feel it as the rest of the infected find him and begin to feast. The spores in their saliva race through his bloodstream, but by the time they take hold there isn't enough left of Jacob to bring back.

Daniel Moore stands from the remains of his son when there's nothing left to eat. He's still hungry, and he knows there are many more meals waiting for him here.

He moves towards the staircase.

I can't believe my luck. One moment I was racing down the hallway in search of the fire escape, and the next I heard a loud bang behind me. I turned around just in time to see a pane of sheet rock fall to the ground, closely followed by a pair of legs. When Vee dropped softly to the ground I could barely believe what I was seeing.

"What the fuck are you doing there?" I demand, half expecting her to vanish like the figment of my imagination I'm sure she is.

Vee dismisses the question with a shake of her head. "Long story, don't worry about it. Did you assholes let a bunch of infected inside?"

Nope, she's real. "Umm... yeah. It was the only way to get you out of here. We needed a distraction to get past the guards."

Vee snaps her head around at the sound of screams in the distance. They're coming from inside the building. "Great distraction, genius. Where are the guys?"

I shrug. "We got separated in the lobby. I think they headed up this way, though. You wanna go look for them?"

She shakes her head. "This place must be twenty floors, we'd never find them. No, Warren knows what he's doing. Soon as he hears those screams he'll know to head for the door. You got a weapon for me?"

"Shit, sorry, I think we left it downstairs." I hold out my Beretta. "You want this back?"

"Uh uh, you keep it," she replies. "I'll make do." She turns to the wall and pulls a fire extinguisher from its bracket, then scans the emergency exit map beside it. "That's where you were headed?" She juts her chin towards the fire escape at the end of the hall. I nod. "No good. I got a look at the fire escape on the way in, and it leads right back to the front of the building. No..." She looks back at the map and points to an exit on the other side of the building. "This one leads across to the parking garage next door. Maybe it's still in one piece."

I look back with dread at the way I came. It leads back towards the lobby staircase.

Worse, it's the direction from which the screams came just a moment ago. I'd rather take my chances climbing down to the infected swarms at the front of the building than head back that way.

"I hope you know what you're doing, Vee. I'll lead the way but watch my back, OK?" I set off along the hallway at a slow jog, and moments later my fears are confirmed. Two men appear on the staircase from above, one running and one tumbling head over heels. The fallen man sprawls on the floor for a moment before regaining his footing, and he continues down towards the lobby just moments before a group of infected race down in pursuit. Vee and I press our backs against the door of the closest room, forcing ourselves into a hiding space just a few inches deep, but the infected don't seem to notice us.

We continue on after a few deep breaths, and as we reach the top of the staircase I risk a look down into the lobby. The two men are nowhere to be seen, but we hear the echo of snarls and screams reverberate across the marble and up the stairs. Something tells me down isn't a good option. Ahead seems clear enough, though, and the fire escape is close. I just pray it's passable. Apart from a few rooms leading off the hallway there would be no escape if we found ourselves trapped down there.

Vee takes the lead, sensing my hesitation, and I quickly follow when I realize I'm out in the open, visible to anyone who might come down the stairs right now. I run to catch up and regain safety in numbers, and I reach her just as she presses her shoulder against the fire escape and pushes open the door.

I catch hold of her just in time, grabbing at the back of her collar as she loses her footing and starts to tumble out the door. She loses her grip on the fire extinguisher, and it falls through the air until it clangs on the asphalt two floors below. The noise attracts a group of infected who look up and begin to snarl and growl at the two of us far above their reach.

The fire escape is gone, sheared away where it should meet the wall. All that's left is the bolts that used to connect it, but beyond them blackened, jagged steel is the only evidence that the staircase was welded until the steel came free.

"Shit!" Vee yells, pulling herself back in through the door. "Fucking idiots could have just blocked it at ground level."

The fire escape used to run down to the narrow alley between the hotel and the parking structure next door, and from the look of the sheared steel on the opposite wall about ten feet away from us it looks like it also served as a walkway connecting the two buildings. Just a few steps or a single leap away, tantalizingly close, the entrance to the garage looks like a wide open mouth. It's a little below us, maybe a couple of feet lower than the hallway, and it looks like we might just be able to make it.

"You think you can make that jump?" Vee asks, already taking a few steps back.

"Ummm... I don't know. Maybe. I'm... shit, I'm not sure."

She pushes me gently aside. "Well, it's either that way or back out the front door, and I don't wanna get eaten today. Just follow my lead, OK? If I can make it so can you." She takes a couple of deep breaths, swings her arms back and forth and breaks into a run towards the door. I barely dare to watch, but I force myself. She leaps from the very edge, thrusting both arms forward as soon as she leaves the ground.

For a moment it looks as if she'll fall far short. I almost yell out, as if there's anything I could possibly do to save her if she missed, but before I can open my mouth her feet connect with the concrete on the other side. She falls forward into a graceful roll, and before I know it she's back on her feet and breathing easy.

"Come on, your turn," she says, beckoning me forward. I feel like my feet are cemented to the ground, but when I hear another scream echo down the hallway behind me I know there's only one real option. I take a few paces back, drop into a runner's starting position and, after a few more seconds of painful indecision, launch myself off the block towards the edge.

"Tom!" I hear the yell from behind me just as my feet are about to leave the ground. It's too late to pull back, and my jump loses power as my mind yells at me to stop and turn. I sail through the air but even before I'm halfway across the chasm it's clear I won't make it all the way.

My ribs bash against the concrete on the other side, knocking the wind out of me, and I start to slip backwards as my weight pulls me over the edge. I scrabble at the ground but there's nothing to grab hold of, and my heart lifts to my throat as I feel myself tip over the edge.

I'm barely even aware of Vee grabbing me by the arm. I don't know what's going on, but I feel my fall arrested just enough that I can scrape from feet against the wall and regain some purchase. I open my eyes, look up and see Vee straining against my weight, her small frame struggling to hold me steady, and from unknown reserves of energy I kick myself up against the wall until I feel the ridge of my aching ribs scrape across the edge and move my weight onto solid ground. I turn and roll, desperately moving until finally I feel the ground beneath my feet.

"Warren, get down here!" I hear Vee yell. I look back at the hotel and see him standing at the open doorway that now seems impossibly distant. It takes me a moment to realize it was Warren yelling my name that distracted me at the crucial moment.

I have no idea how we both made it across, and I don't dare take a breath as Warren takes just a few short steps back, sprints forward and athletically leaps across the gap. He lands a solid two feet into the garage, as if the gap was nothing but an easy step.

"Where's Bishop?" I ask, struggling to catch my breath. Warren frowns and looks down at me.

"Fuck, I thought he was with you. How did you lose track of him?"

I feel the anger rise. "I didn't fucking lose track of him. I thought the two of you had left me!"

"OK, OK, no point in us bouncing each other off the walls," Warren replies, trying to calm us both. "What are we gonna do? We can't just leave him in there. He's not even armed."

I look back at the door we jumped from. There's no way any of us could ever make it back. It's a good two feet higher than us, and it'd take a superhuman effort to reach it without falling. Besides that, even if we could leap over and grab the frame before falling the wall is covered in jagged steel from the destroyed fire escape. We'd be stabbed for sure.

It's a few seconds before I register the sound of the footsteps. Loud, heavy clomps bouncing off the walls of the alleyway like a slow drumbeat, followed soon enough by deep, panting breaths.

Bishop appears at the door on the other side of the alley, and he scans around for a moment before he notices us on the other side. Before he speaks a word his eyes catch the long drop to the ground below, and his face turns white. "Oh, fuck," he sighs, looking like he's on the edge of tears. "I can't jump that far, you guys."

I pull myself to my feet and call out to him across the void. "You can, Bishop. I thought the same thing but I made it." I don't mention that I almost didn't. "It looks further than it is. Just take a good run up and then throw yourself across. Come on, buddy, you have to try."

Bishop's eyes well with tears, but he seems to trust me. He wipes his eyes and nods. "OK, I'll try. Just gimme a second to get ready for it, OK?"

The shot comes out of nowhere. We all hear it, but we all look in different directions. Vee and Warren look down into the alleyway and I look behind me back into the garage, but it's not until we see Bishop that we learn the truth.

The big guy looks down at his chest, at the dirty fatigues he's been wearing for days. It's hard to see against the dark camo, but a growing patch of blood spreads across his jacket like a blooming flower.

"Oh," he says simply, his voice little more than a whisper. He touches his jacket and his hand comes away red before he plants it against the door frame to support himself. His legs tremble for a moment, and without another sound he falls slowly forward and tumbles face first into the alleyway.

In the alley beneath the snarls grow louder as Bishop lands hard on a dumpster, rolls off and tumbles into the middle of the pack. Before we can tell if he's alive or dead they close in over him, grabbing at his clothes and tugging at his arms and legs. I pray the fall killed him, but as the infected loom over him I hear a weak, desperate whimper. A gap forms between his attackers, and for a moment I see Bishop's eyes, wide open and terrified. I may be imagining it but he seems to meet my gaze.

I don't take the time to think. I already know what needs to be done. I take a tight grip on my Beretta, point it down at the alley and squeeze the trigger, putting a lucky shot through Bishop's cheek. I won't let him return as one of those things.

For a moment there's a stunned silence. None of us wants to be the first to speak. We wouldn't know what to say. We're just numb.

So numb that it occurs to none of us that whoever shot Bishop may still be here.

Almost in slow motion Warren drops to the ground as I watch. His mouth opens wide with shock, and it takes a moment for me to realize he's taken a hit in the leg. Vee thinks more quickly than me, and before he hits the deck she grabs him and drags him away from the entrance, behind the cover of a parked car.

I look up, and I suddenly feel like I'm in a nightmare I've had a dozen times over. The shooter stands above me and across the alleyway, grinning, a pistol in his hand. I watch as he calmly reloads as if he's completely unconcerned that we pose a threat.

Without any conscious thought at all I lift my hand, point my Beretta at the door and squeeze off shots until the magazine is empty. The man ducks quickly back inside at the first shot, and every one of my bullets buries itself harmlessly in the drywall of the hallway.

My arm drops to my side, and I stare at the empty door. My mind is barely working at half speed, and I don't even try to resist when Vee grabs me by the collar and drags me behind the car. It doesn't matter. None of this could possibly be real.

"Fucking *wake up*, Tom!" she yells, slapping me in the face. "You have to help me with Warren!"

I move as if I'm in a trance. Vee hooks an arm beneath one of Warren's shoulders and I do the same, pulling him away deeper into the garage as he grits his teeth through the pain. It's not until we all collapse, exhausted, at the far end of the structure that I begin to wake up.

"That fucking asshole, I'm gonna take his balls!" Vee exclaims, punching a car door.

Warren pushes himself painfully up until he's sitting up against the side of the car. He grabs at his trouser leg and tears it to the knee, inspecting the wound. He feels the back of his calf and sighs. "Through and through, I'll live. Now who the fuck was that?"

Vee hisses through clenched teeth. "He calls himself the Chief. He's the fucker who locked me up. Wanted to use me as a sex toy for his little fucking group. I'm gonna kill him."

I hear my own voice, but I'm barely aware I'm speaking. It still feels like a dream, and I can't quite believe what I just saw.

"His name isn't the Chief." I look back across the garage to the hotel as if I might still see him standing there smiling in the doorway. "And you're not going to kill him, Vee. I am."

Vee looks at me as if I've lost it. "What are you talking about? That's the fucker who runs the place. Calls himself the Chief."

I shake my head. "I know him by a different name." I look down at my spent gun and wish I had more ammo. If I had the fucking nuclear codes in front of me I'd use them if it meant he'd be dead. "His name is Sergeant Laurence," I say, staring back at the hotel. "I met him in New York. He's the man who killed my girlfriend. Shot her in the chest and drove over her body."

I look back at Vee, and she can tell by the fire in my eyes that I'm completely sane, and completely serious. "And now he's killed Bishop. Enough." I nod towards Warren's injured leg. "We're going to get Warren's leg fixed up, then we're going to find more ammo. Then I'm going to kill that bastard."

In the distance I hear the howls of the infected echo from the streets below. For a month those sounds have stuck terror in my heart and sent me cowering into the shadows. Not any more. Now the dead will become my allies, bound by a shared cause.

There are worse things out there than the infected.

And I'm going to kill them all.

Thank you for reading CORDYCEPS, the second book in the Last Man Standing series. If you'd like to keep updated with my latest releases and sales you should subscribe to my newsletter:

https://app.mailerlite.com/webforms/landing/y1i5k1

or follow me on Facebook:

https://www.facebook.com/keithtaylorauthor

Thanks!

Made in the USA
San Bernardino, CA
20 November 2016